THE FLYING BOYS TO THE RESCUE

EDWARD S. ELLIS

Originally published in 1911

THE FLYING BOYS SERIES

TABLE OF CONTENTS

CHAPTER I
SEEKING A CLUE

HARVEY HAMILTON, the young aviator, found himself in the most distressful dilemma of his life. He and his devoted friend, the colored youth Bohunkus Johnson, had left their homes near the New Jersey village of Mootsport, and sailing away in the former's aeroplane had run into a series of adventures in eastern Pennsylvania, which have been related in "The Flying Boys in the Sky." It was the good fortune of Harvey to help in the recovery of the little girl who was kidnapped from her home in Philadelphia some weeks before. All having gone well down to the time of her rescue, he was awaiting the return of "Bunk" to continue their outing, when to his consternation he learned that his dusky comrade had gone off with Professor Milo Morgan in his unique monoplane, which bore the fantastic name "The Dragon of the Skies." To add to the annoyance of the situation, the couple had started on the maddest enterprise of which a mortal has ever been guilty,—a trip across the Atlantic Ocean to the continent of Africa. That fact of itself would have stamped the gaunt, grizzled aviator as the veriest lunatic outside of a hospital for the insane.

Two remembrances caused Harvey Hamilton keen regret: one was his hasty words to Bunk, which were the indirect cause of this astounding venture, and the other his failure to warn him of the mental weakness of Professor Morgan. Had he done as he ought to have done, in either instance, the lad would have been saved from the terrifying peril into which he had rushed.

But while our young friend condemned himself without stint, it was now too late for mere grief. The momentous question was whether he could do anything to save Bunk, and if so, how should he go about it?

The Dragon of the Skies was not only much swifter than his biplane, but it had a start of at least two days. If the owner had headed for the Dark Continent, he was already well advanced upon the fateful journey. In that event Harvey could do nothing but wait through the long days and weeks for the news that might never come to him.

The more he strode up and down the hotel porch and thought of the matter, the more he was puzzled. He must attempt nothing without good counsel and the best man to give it was Simmons Pendar, the detective, who had been the means of rescuing little Grace Hastings from the band of kidnappers. Although inaction was torture, he stayed in Chesterton, with his aeroplane in the primitive hangar, until Pendar, having finished the rush of business, found time to greet him. When Harvey asked him for a few minutes, the officer, who naturally was in high spirits, replied in his hearty manner:

"My dear boy, you shall have all the time you want; I can never forget the obligations under which you have placed the Hastings and me; let me know how I can serve you."

They seated themselves at the farther end of the porch, beyond earshot of eavesdroppers and talked in low tones. It took Harvey only a short time to tell his story. The detective whistled softly when he finished.

"Well, this is a peculiar situation indeed. Neither of us ever dreamed of anything of the kind. You are asking yourself whether you can do anything to help your friend?"

"Is it possible for me to lift a hand for him?"

"I hope so."

"There's mighty little comfort in those words, Mr. Pendar."

"Would it cheer you more if I said there was no hope at all?"

"I am afraid it would not make much difference in my feelings. I cannot remain idle, but I don't know which way to turn or what to do."

The detective proved his power of quick thinking and of concentrating his faculties upon any theme that might claim them, by saying in his positive manner:

"In the first place, I don't believe Professor Morgan has started for Africa."

Harvey Hamilton almost sprang from his chair.

"Why do you say that, after what we have learned?"

"I may be wrong, but I am strongly of the opinion that while he has in mind such a trip he isn't prepared to try it just yet. No mistake about it, he is a wonderful inventor. He has already done enough to make him wealthy and famous. He courses through the air without noise; he can go straight aloft by means of his uplifter, which enables him to hover stationary like a bird over any spot he selects. From a remark I once heard him make, I believe the great idea upon which he is working is that of drawing electricity from the air and using it as motive power. When he is able to do that—and who shall say that he will not solve the problem very soon?—he can stay aloft indefinitely; that is, until he uses up his supply of food and oil."

"He has already formulated a chemical composition that will keep him aloft for half a day."

"Not long enough to cross the Atlantic. He is figuring on his scheme now, and time and experiment are necessary for him to reach success."

"He is likely to make a mistake, is he not?"

"Being human, though crazy, he will do that. But there is a method in his madness. Having accomplished several remarkable things, he has proved that thus far all has gone right with him. Now, my dear boy, while he is sure he will sooner or later cross the Atlantic, he will not start till he is ready and his machine fit. Therefore, I repeat that days and perhaps weeks will pass before he makes the attempt of which other aviators are still dreaming."

"And what will he do in the meantime?"

Detective Pendar shrugged his shoulders.

"Experiment."

"You encourage me by what you say, but from what point is he likely to start?"

"Naturally where the width of the ocean is narrowest. He will not leave the New Jersey or New York or New England coast, but in my judgment will bid North America good-bye at Quebec or its neighborhood and head directly eastward for Liverpool."

"What is the distance between those two cities?"

"Twenty-six hundred miles. Say he can average seventy-five miles an hour."

The detective did a little mental figuring.

"If he can do that and has no accident, he will reach Liverpool in one day and a half after leaving Quebec. If he can make a hundred miles an hour — and depend upon it the aviators of the near future will surpass that speed — he can bid Canada good-bye in the afternoon and watch the sun set in England on the following day."

"When at Liverpool he will still be a long way from Africa."

"But the after trip will be mainly by land. The Channel has already been frequently crossed by air men and when he follows suit he will be on the continent. Then it will be a pleasing excursion southward over France and Spain to Gibraltar, from which it is only a step to Africa. Have you any idea in what part of the Dark Continent your colored friend expects to find his distinguished parent?"

"I have no more idea than he has himself, but I should think it is well to the south."

"That route would take him through Morocco, Rio de Oro, Senegal, to Liberia, with the larger half of Africa still to the southward. But it is idle to speculate on their course after crossing the ocean, a feat they are not likely to accomplish for some time to come. Let us figure on what they will probably do while in our own country."

"That is the great question. If we can't head off the lunatic and rescue poor Bunk before he turns his back upon these shores he will never be rescued at all."

"Professor Morgan is a moody man. Only on rare occasions does he come out of his shell, as he did on the night when he first called upon you at the home of the countryman."

"When we met afterward he was hardly willing to look at, much less speak to me."

"That is his natural frame of mind; now and then the reaction hits him, when he will admit there are other human beings on our earth. It is useless, therefore, to look for the Professor in any of the cities or towns. He will not share his secrets with others, but will push his investigations in private and far from the haunts of men. I believe he will locate somewhere to the northward, either in the mountainous regions of New York, New England or Canada, so that when he is prepared, he will have only a short distance to go to get to his starting point. But," added Detective Pendar, "we are in the realm of guesswork and that part of the earth lying yonder" (he made a sweep of his arm to the northward) "is pretty big. Of course you will never find him without first picking up some clue."

"And how shall that be done?"

"Ah, I wish I could answer."

The detective lighted another cigar, leaned back in his chair with his legs crossed and puffed awhile in silence. He was thinking hard and his listener waited for him to speak.

"I have been trying to decide upon what fact I base a vague belief that this loon has his workshop in the northern part of New York State, well toward the Canadian border. He never told me anything about himself and I have not seen his name or doings in print. The impression must be one of those hazy ones that steal into the brain without any apparent reason, and are explained by some as due to a sixth sense."

"Such as when you located the kidnappers in this part of the world," ventured Harvey Hamilton.

"That was quite different; I accidentally ran upon a definite clue, but there is nothing of the kind in sight here. You have no idea how many of the successes among us detectives are due to lucky accidents. Now such an original genius as Milo Morgan cannot always keep out of the public eye. His achievements are so remarkable that several of them must become known; the omni-present reporters will hunt him up; if they can get snapshots his picture will appear on the printed page, with interesting interviews, all probably faked. If this does not occur, his doings will be mentioned in some journal; if you will arrange with a press-clipping bureau, you will probably get the clue you need."

Harvey had never thought of anything like this. It added to his hopefulness and he began to believe it quite possible that Bohunkus Johnson might be run down and saved from what seemed impending death.

"The character of Professor Morgan being what it is, why was he willing to take my colored friend with him?"

"It was not altogether the whim of a lunatic. He could not have failed to note that the negro is stupid, consequently would not bore him with questions which he did not wish to answer. At the same time, Bunk is big, powerful and good-natured, — in short an ideal assistant, for there must be arduous labor connected with the experiments of the brilliant inventor. In my judgment it was these facts which influenced Morgan to take the lad with him; Bunk would be desirable for the same reasons on a trip across the ocean and it would be an easy reward to give him for his help."

"It seems to me, Mr. Pendar, that valuable time will be lost while waiting for news through the sources you name."

"Possibly you are right, but I can think of no other way that promises success. From Chesterton you will first go to your home; you can reach there to-morrow; you will tell your father everything of course, and he will be as helpful as he was in getting you a new aeroplane."

"How?"

"When he returns to New York he can telephone the leading press-clipping bureaus and not only set them on the watch for future bits of information, but have them hunt for that which has been published lately. Something will be picked up quite soon and then your real work will begin."

"What course do you advise me to follow?"

"Go to Albany or Troy, or even farther north, making sure your father knows where to reach you by telegraph. As soon as he receives the information he wants, he can wire it to you and then you will have to depend upon your own wits. I shall venture upon a few more words of advice. Have you had much experience in revolver shooting?"

"No; I have a fine Colt's at home and my brother Dick has one, and we sometimes try our skill at targets, but he prefers a rifle or shotgun, and I don't particularly care for either."

"You may not need any firearms, but don't forget to take your pistol and a fair supply of cartridges with you. As they say out West, you don't often want a revolver, but when you do, you want it blanked bad. It will be well also to supply yourself pretty liberally with funds, for there's no saying what necessity you will run against."

"I shall not forget your counsel; I appreciate it and shall follow it in spirit and letter."

"I wish I could go with you, but I am not my own master. You have my address and will inform me when you have any news to tell."

The two shook hands and separated.

CHAPTER II
A REMARKABLE LETTER

SEATED on the broad veranda of his home at Mootsport, in the soft summer moonlight, with his father, mother, sister Mildred and Mr. Hartley grouped around him, Harvey Hamilton told the story of his aerial trip to Chesterton in eastern Pennsylvania. All listened intently to the account of the rescue of little Grace Hastings from the Black Hand kidnappers, followed by the strange disappearance of Bohunkus Johnson in the company of the cranky Professor Morgan.

They had read of the former event in the newspapers, but their interest naturally centered upon Bunk, for whom each felt a warm regard. It is not worth while to set down all that was said, the conclusion of which was summed up by the merchant:

"The advice of your detective friend is good, Harvey, and you must follow it to the letter. I shall set the clipping bureaus to work as soon as I reach the city to-morrow morning. You will go by train to the Ten Eyck House in Albany and wait there for a telegram from me. I feel sure you will not have to wait long. The curious fact in this affair is that within the last two or three days I read an item about a wonderful inventor who traveled through the air without noise and could remain stationary as long as he wished."

"Can you remember the particulars?" eagerly asked his son.

"I have been trying to do so but am unable. It was only one of the many references to flying machines with which the papers are filled. Whatever I might recall would be misleading, so it is better to let it go. Some of those wide-awake people will speedily unearth the facts, and I shall lose no time in sending them to you. I can telephone the agencies and have them begin at once."

Thus it came about that the next evening found our young friend in the sitting-room of the Ten Eyck, the fashionable hotel in the capital of the State. The weather had turned chilly, with a drizzling mist which made the warmth within pleasant, even though it was the sultry season of the year. It is tedious to await the deferred coming of a friend or the happening of some expected event. Harvey had gaped and yawned and glanced through most of the metropolitan dailies in the reading-room, weakly hoping to run across reference to the subject that engrossed his mind, but he found nothing and decided that he must depend upon his father for the information needed.

He finished his evening meal, returned to the sitting-room and a few minutes later received the expected message. It was so full that it is better to summarize what it said:

Professor Milo Morgan was referred to as the coming Edison of aviation. He had perfected a number of amazing inventions, such as a noiseless monoplane that could be held motionless at will, and was capable of a speed of nearly a hundred miles an hour. The Professor was able to remain above the earth for twelve hours. As soon as he could triple this period he would start on an aerial voyage from Quebec to Liverpool. He was not quite ready to do so, but was certain that a few days or possibly a week or two would see the marvelous feat accomplished. He had sailed over several of the States and gone as far south as the Carolinas. His first intention was to cross the Rockies and visit the Pacific coast, but he had decided to travel in the opposite direction. The Professor's workshop was somewhere in Essex

County, northern New York, but he kept the exact location a profound secret because he did not wish to be annoyed by visitors and reporters.

"In Essex County are the Adirondacks, where brother Dick is camping out with his friends," reflected Harvey; "it is the close season, so they daren't disturb deer and other big game, but they are having plenty of fun. Now if I could locate the workshop of the Professor I should be able to do something for Bunk."

Aye, there was the rub. As we know, the Adirondacks cover a large area, so large indeed that many a hunter has lost his way among the solitudes and died of starvation and exposure. A person might spend months in searching for another, and unless he had some clue never gain a glimpse of him. It would be the wildest folly for Harvey Hamilton to try to trace the Professor without more enlightenment than thus far he possessed.

The only information of value in the long telegram was that the inventor made his home in the large county, most of which lies to the westward of Lake Champlain. It seemed reasonable to believe that he was there at that time putting the finishing touches to his machine, but so far as finding him was concerned he might as well have been in the heart of Canada or far out over the boisterous Atlantic.

It will be recalled that Detective Pendar insisted that many of the most brilliant successes in his profession were due to accidental or trifling incidents. Never did this truth receive a more striking illustration than in the case of Harvey Hamilton, within the same hour in which he read the first telegram from his father. He had laid the yellow sheets on the table in front of him and was trying to figure out what he should do, when one of the bellboys, in obedience to an order of the clerk at the desk, handed him a second lengthy message, which like the former was from his parent. It said:

"A letter has just arrived from Bunk addressed to you. It is without town or date, but the postmark on the outside is 'Dawson, N. Y,', and it was stamped yesterday. You can readily locate the place as I haven't the time to do so. I had to get Mildred to help me translate Bunk's spelling and sentences, but we finally succeeded and here is the result:

"'Dear Harv,—I hope you are well, because I am. Have had a bully time, but the Professor isn't quite ready to start for Africa. He will do so in a few days. He treats me well, but sometimes he acts blamed queer. I guess that is because he feels sort of scared about meeting so great a man as my father, the Chief Foozleum. He told me not to write to anybody at all because he didn't wish any one to know where we are. He has gone off for a little while and I take the chance to write you, for I know you would like to hear from me and I can get a chance to mail it when he isn't around. He must think I'm a chump not to know how to write a letter without blabbing a secret. I can keep things to myself as well as anybody. If you'd give me a thousand dollars I wouldn't let you know that we have a cabin in the woods near Dawson. No, sir; you can't fool me; I'm mum every time. My next letter will be from Africa and written in the palace of Chief Foozleum.

"'No more at present. Your loving friend,

"'Bunk.'"

Yielding to his first impulse Harvey Hamilton threw back his head and laughed till the tears came.

"Bless your heart, Bunk! What should I do without you? No more loyal heart ever beat than yours. I can't blame you for giving me the slip as you did, and it is natural that you should be filled with the scheme of an aerial voyage across the Atlantic. If I can succeed in saving you from the attempt, it will be through the help which in the innocence of your heart you gave me."

Manifestly the first thing to be done was to find where the town of Dawson is situate. Harvey had never heard of it, and in his perplexity he applied to the clerk, who was not only courteous but well informed. Pondering a moment, he replied:

"Dawson is a small town, though large enough to support a newspaper, two churches and a public school. It is in Warren County, well up to the north and not far from Essex."

"Then it is near the Adirondack region?"

"It may be said to be in it. Mount Gore, a part of Schroon Lake, and several spurs of the Adirondacks are in Warren, though you must travel pretty well up into Essex to reach the heart of the mountain district. Do you think of visiting the section?"

"That is my purpose."

"Don't forget that the open season for deer is from September 16 to November 1, with the chances that half a dozen amateurs will take you for big game and plug you before you get a hundred yards from camp."

"I have no thought of hunting except for a person who I have reason to believe is near the town of Dawson. Can you tell me how I can best reach the place?"

"Go by rail to Beelsburg, where you will meet a stage that makes the daily trip from and to Dawson."

"How long is the stage ride?"

"It is called ten miles, but it is more. The road is rough with a good many hills and bad places. The journey takes nearly three hours each way."

"Can you inform me when I should leave Albany to reach Dawson on the same day?"

The clerk had to consult the time tables before answering this question. It took only a brief while to fish out what he sought.

"It is eighty-four miles by rail with one change of cars at Thurston, where you have to wait twenty minutes. Leaving Albany at eight-thirty, you reach Beelsburg in time for a midday dinner, after which comes a jolt of a dozen miles to Dawson. The doctors tell us that a vigorous shaking up is good for digestion, so when you reach Dawson you ought to be ready for another square meal."

Harvey could not ask for more explicit directions, and thanking the clerk for his kindness, he went to his room. In the morning he sent a telegram to his father's office explaining his plans and expressing hope of success. The programme as outlined in the conversation between Harvey and the hotel clerk was followed. Arriving at Beelsburg on time, Harvey ate his noon meal at that station, after which he and two passengers had a tedious wait for the stage which ought to have arrived from Dawson an hour before the train. When at last the lumbering vehicle swung round the corner and drew up at the station platform, the explanation of the delay was prosaic. An axle had broken and the driver had patched it up until he reached the wheelwright shop at the other end of the village, where a longer time was needed to mend the fracture.

Harvey's fellow-passengers were middle-aged men and neighbors who had much to say to each other. What he overheard was of no interest to him. Once or twice he was on the point of asking questions about Professor Morgan, but they showed no sociability toward him, and a feeling of distrust held him mute upon the one subject that filled his thoughts. He decided that it was prudent to await his arrival in the country town.

Harvey found the dozen-mile ride all that was pictured by the hotel clerk of the Ten Eyck House. For most of the way the gaunt horses walked, except when going down-hill, and in many places it was hard pulling for them. But nothing of note happened, and as it was growing dark, the stage halted in front of the Washington House and Harvey, with traveling bag in hand, sprang out. The others remained in order to ride to their homes farther down the street.

The hotel, with its rather high-sounding title, was a small, modest structure, as was to be expected where the guests were scant and far between. The young aviator had no trouble in obtaining a comfortable room. Had he been accompanied by a dozen friends, they would have been accommodated with the same promptness.

He had decided upon doing as he did in Albany, that is, question the clerk of the hotel, who it might be reasonably supposed would have a wide acquaintance with the affairs of the neighborhood. But a difficulty appeared at the outset: the primitive hotel had no clerk. The landlord, a large, beefy, slow-witted man, who wheezed when he waddled about and seldom spoke unless spoken to, and not always then, managed affairs, and sat at the head of the table during meals. He showed not the slightest interest in his solitary guest, but filled and sent his plate to him by the hands of a tidy young woman who evidently was his daughter.

Since, however, the Boniface seemed to be the only available source of information, Harvey wasted no time. The dining-room being empty of all except the two, he finished his meal first, and walking beside the table to its head, sat down in a chair near the phthisical landlord, who glared at him from under his shaggy brows as if he failed to understand the meaning of the movement.

"If you please," opened the guest, "I should like to ask you a few questions."

The host kept on eating, but grunted a response which the young man accepted as permission to proceed.

CHAPTER III
A WORKSHOP IN THE WOODS

THE brief conversation that followed was unique.

"I am looking for Professor Morgan," said Harvey by way of setting the ball rolling. The landlord thrust a big piece of meat in his mouth and continued chewing, but a side glance showed he had heard the words.

"Do you know him?" continued Harvey.

"Is he the chap that's got a shop about a half a mile out in the woods, where he makes airships?" asked the host in turn.

"That's the man! What can you tell me about him?"

"I never heerd of him; can't tell you nothing."

"Then how do you know his workshop is half a mile out in the woods?"

Harvey Hamilton had a quick temper and resented the manner of the other.

"I don't; I asked you if he's the chap."

"What chap?"

"The one that has a shop a half mile away, where he makes airships."

"How do you know he does?"

"See here, young man," said the landlord, so nettled that he suspended mastication for the moment and looked threateningly at his questioner; "you're getting too flip; I didn't say that long-legged galoot does nothing of the kind; I asked you if he did."

"And I answer that of all fools that pretend to have a grain of sense you're entitled to the medal."

And with flushed face Harvey sprang from his chair, stalked out of the room and banged the door behind him. Perhaps he should not have been so rude, but surely he had great provocation. Undecided what he ought to do next, he went upstairs to his room. Dawson had not yet risen to the dignity of gas, but he lighted the kerosene lamp that stood on the little bureau, and sat down in one of the two chairs with which his apartment was furnished.

"It's provoking that I should hit upon the biggest chump in this place to question, when probably every one else could tell me what I want to know — Come in!"

The last was in response to a knock on the door, which was pushed open the next moment, and the young woman who had served in the dining-room stepped within.

"Good evening," she said to the surprised Harvey, who politely rose to his feet; "you know I waited on the table."

"I remember you; I am at your service."

"I was standing just outside the door that goes to the kitchen and I heerd everything you said to paw and what he said to you."

"I got very little satisfaction from him," remarked Harvey, ashamed of his hasty words at that time; "and am afraid I lost my temper."

"You mustn't mind paw, that's a way he has. He thinks it isn't right to tell a stranger anything about folks that have been guests at our hotel."

Harvey saw that here was the well of the information he sought. He asked the young woman to take the chair near the door, while he resumed his own seat. She complied without any false pretense of modesty. Being chambermaid, there was nothing to criticise in her action.

"I gather from what you just said that Professor Morgan has stayed at your hotel?"

"He never stopped over night, but he has eat a good many meals in our house; he took dinner here to-day."

"How long has he made his headquarters in this part of the country?"

She reflected a moment.

"He come here last fall, that is, to stay. But for weeks before that he had been sending all sorts of stuff,—wheels, cranks, knives, engines, pieces of machinery and lots of things the like of which I have never saw, and they was carted out into the woods, where he hired some carpenters to put up a big cabin, and a still bigger one that ain't very high where he stowed his flying machine and other things."

"And he has made his home there ever since?"

"I 'spose you might say so, though he's away a good deal; sometimes he's gone for weeks afore he shows up agin."

"How long has he been able to fly with his machine?"

"I can't say for certain, but the first time I seen him was last spring—April, I think—when he sailed over the town and we didn't see him agin for more'n a week."

"Where is his shop?"

"You walk down the main street to the second turn, then foller a road that ain't much traveled, for about a quarter of a mile; then you turn to the left over a hunter's trail that has been there ever since any one can remember, and keep along that till you run aginst his cabin."

The young woman, who announced that her name was Ann Harbor, illustrated her explanations by so many gestures that her listener was sure he could readily trace the eccentric inventor to his retreat.

"You say he ate dinner at your hotel to-day?"

"Yes."

"You mean him and the young colored man with him."

Ann's big gray eyes became bigger with surprise.

"He didn't have any colored person with him."

"But you have seen them together within the last few days?"

The young woman gravely shook her head.

"Professor Morgan is the strangest man I ever have saw; he has been here a good many times but never spoke a word to me, and I don't believe he's said a half dozen words to paw; he never brought any person to the hotel and I've never saw a colored boy with him."

"Have you ever been to his place in the woods?"

"No; folks say he won't let anyone come nigh it; if a person does so he has some contraption that will blow him into the sky; you don't catch me running such a resk."

Harvey Hamilton's heart sank within him. The fact that Professor Morgan had come alone to this house for his meals had a sinister meaning as regarded Bohunkus, whose appetite was something which could be soothed only in the way nature intended.

Had the lunatic discovered that Bunk sent a letter to his friend, and had he punished him for it? Was he starving the poor fellow to death, or had he taken quicker means of ridding himself of his company? Had he turned him adrift, dropped him from his airship, or chosen one of a score of methods for wiping the lad out of existence?

Such and similar were the questions that rushed through the brain of Harvey as he held converse with the young woman. While by no means ready to give up hope, he felt that the outlook for his friend could not well be much darker.

Since his caller had nothing further of importance to impart, she bade him good-night and thanked him for the liberal tip he gave her.

"I'll say nothing to your father of what you have told me," he promised, as she rose to go.

"You can tell him all you wanter; I don't care what paw thinks about it."

"There is no need of disclosing anything and I don't believe he wishes to talk with me after our spat this evening in the dining-room."

The night was unusually chilly for the season, but the sky showed signs of clearing. Harvey was hopeful that the morrow would be pleasant, although the country which he had entered lies so far north and is so elevated that he found a marked difference between its temperature and that of his own home. It was on the edge of the Adirondack region famous throughout the Union, and so great an attraction that some of its annual visitors come from across the ocean.

His plan was to go to the headquarters of Professor Morgan, tell Bunk the real situation and compel him to return to his home in New Jersey. The actual problem he would have to face was the inventor, who was likely to interpose and probably forbid any action of the kind.

"I am glad I brought my revolver," reflected the youth, as he lay in bed waiting for slumber to close his eyelids; "I pray that I shall never have to use it, but it may prove the only means of saving Bunk and perhaps myself."

When he awoke in the morning he was delighted to find that the day was an ideal one. The sun was shining brightly, the sky was free of clouds and the air mild, but with the crispness peculiar to that remarkable section of our country. The landlord did not appear at the breakfast table, but remained in his office smoking a big briarwood pipe, from which fact Harvey decided that he had already broken fast. His daughter Ann did the honors, and the remembrance of the tip of the night before made her do her best to please the guest. When she had set down a plate of hot griddlecakes and a cup of steaming coffee, she said:

"Professor Morgan was here last night when you and me was talking up-stairs."

"Did he have the negro lad with him?" asked the astonished Harvey.

"He was alone like he always is; he and paw had a talk."

"I suppose your father told him I was here."

"I don't know a word that either said; I asked paw and he told me it was none of my business; but I guess paw told him all you and him spoke."

"Well, I don't see that any harm was done, for the Professor would learn it when I called upon him."

"La sakes! you ain't going out to that awful place, be you?"

"That's what I mean to do."

"Look out you don't git blowed sky high."

"I shan't forget your warning."

"Will you be back to dinner?"

"I am not sure, but I hope to see you again before I leave this part of the country."

"If you go into the mountains look out for bears and deers."

Harvey assured her that he would do his best to follow her counsel. There could be no doubt that his douceur had done good work.

His first impulse was to say a few pleasant words to the landlord, as a sort of an apology for the little misunderstanding of the night before, but the man looked so sour that he feared another snubbing and let him alone.

Directly after breakfast, therefore, the guest stepped off the porch and started along the principal street, but purposely took a direction opposite to that named by Ann Harbor. Having gone a few rods, he turned about and followed the right course. He resorted to this little subterfuge in order to learn whether the landlord felt any curiosity as to his movements, and the trick worked. The man had come out of his office, and still smoking his briarwood, was watching him. He knew of course that the youth was on his way to the retreat of Professor Morgan.

"They discussed me last night. All of the landlord's sympathies are with the crank, so I can count on no aid from him. It is well for a person to know how he stands with his acquaintances."

Ann's directions were so clear that Harvey could not err. He followed the street, took the turn named, and finally struck the trail that led straight to his destination. He was impressed by the abrupt change in the character of the country. A few steps seemed to have taken him from a settled section to the primitive wilderness. The ground rose steeply, rocks abounded, and the path wound in and out among pines which stood like sentinels guarding the approach to the forbidden spot beyond. He pressed on, walking slowly, with eyes and ears alert, listening and watching for whatever might occur.

"I wonder what the Professor and Bunk will say when I walk in on them. I have been told that the safest course with a lunatic is not to show any fear of him. If you keep cool you can bluff it through with the most violent — hello! here we are!"

He had passed around a mass of boulders which towered twenty-odd feet above his head and had come in sight of the structure for which he was hunting. His first impression was regarding its ordinary appearance, for it might be taken for the home of some poor dweller in the woods. It was a log cabin recalling that in which he had spent an evening with Abisha Wharton in the Pennsylvania solitudes, where he first met Professor Morgan. There were the two windows with the door and small porch between, the half-story above, and the stone chimney on the outside at the gable end. The open space in front was smaller than that of the other cabin, and not the first attempt had been made at cultivation. The owner's interest lay wholly inside. Harvey noticed one significant fact: the windows, instead of consisting of a number of small panes, had each a big plate of glass for the upper and a similar one for the lower sash. This was probably with a view of improving the light. From where the youth stood he caught a glimpse of innumerable appliances, such as wheels, rubber tires, coils of wire, tools and strange models, which hung upon hooks or stood on shelves; the top of a lathe showed, though his view was imperfect.

A broad low flat building to the right was the hangar for the "Dragon of the Skies," but he saw the front was open and the remarkable monoplane was not in sight; nor did he gain a glimpse of the man or colored youth. While debating as to what was best to do, he caught sight of a square of white paper pinned on the door. Going forward he read:

"WARNING!

"All trespassers are warned that any attempt to enter this building without invitation from me will cause their instant death. The electrical apparatus cannot be avoided and it strikes with the suddenness of a bolt from heaven.

"The undersigned starts this morning for a distant country and will not return for several weeks. When he does so, the presence or absence of dead bodies in front of this door will inform him whether any one or more or none at all has dared to disregard my notice. It will be equally futile for any one to try to follow me.

"M. MORGAN."

CHAPTER IV
THE BIPLANE IN ACTION

HARVEY HAMILTON read the strange "Warning" twice through, by which time every sentence and word were imbedded in his memory. I am glad to say that in one respect he showed common sense: he did not venture a step farther upon forbidden ground. He was tempted to try the door or windows or to explore the premises, but the chances were a hundred to one that Professor Morgan said no more than the simple truth in the pencilled notice tacked upon the oaken door of the cabin.

Possibly it was a violation of that law which forbids a person to use a trap gun in guarding his property against burglars, but if so, the fact itself remained. The person who attempted to force an entrance would undoubtedly run into some infernal contrivance that would instantly blot him out of existence. Consequently, instead of advancing, the youth withdrew several paces where he knew he was safe. He was still near enough to read the ominous words had it been necessary, but he could not forget them.

During the brief while in which he thought upon their meaning, Harvey did a bit of reasoning that would have been a credit to Detective Simmons Pendar himself.

"That notice is meant for me. The Professor learned last night that I was at the hotel and he needed no one to tell him my business. The closing sentence is intended to check any pursuit by me. His statement that he has started for a distant country to be gone several weeks is also a bit of information for my exclusive benefit. He doesn't name Africa, but that is the destination in his mind.

"Why didn't he take Bunk to the hotel for his meals? Evidently he feared to trust him, suspecting he would write to me, as the Professor may have learned he had already done. Although Ann did not tell me and likely did not know it, he has brought the necessary food to this place. He forbade Bunk to stray from the cabin, and the fellow was so scared by the words and manner of the Professor that he dared not disobey him.

"Why is he so resolute that I shall not prevent Bunk from going on a trip which only the brain of a lunatic could originate? Bunk, in his first feeling of resentment toward me, won the sympathy of this strange person, who, as Detective Pendar said, saw how useful my friend would be as his assistant. Had Bunk wished to leave him at the beginning of their venture, the Professor might have consented, but the poor lad is as eager as he for the trip. The inventor is angered against me because I am trying to interfere, and is resolute I shall not succeed. His disordered brain has settled into an iron resolve that I shall be defeated at every cost. Until I can bring about some understanding with Bunk and make an ally of him, I have the biggest kind of a job on my hands, but with the help of Heaven it shall be pushed through to the end."

One phase of the situation gave Harvey a new thrill of hope. Professor Morgan on his visit to the hotel the night before must have learned that the young aviator had come to Dawson by train and stage, leaving his aeroplane behind. Naturally he would conclude that his pursuer meant to make no further use of the machine. Harvey's manifest course therefore was to turn to his aerocar to solve the problem.

"I shall go home as fast as steam can carry me and return faster than it can bring me to this point and it will then be do or die."

The perplexing problem was to guess what course the crazy inventor would follow from that morning when he, with Bunk as his companion, had sailed into the northern skies. Was he really heading for Quebec or some distant point that would shorten the distance across the Atlantic, with the purpose of striking out upon his crazy venture, or was he subjecting his machine to a crucial test before doing so?

Whatever might be the intention of Professor Morgan, it was evident that he could not escape that test, for previous to plunging into the aerial ocean to the eastward, he must sail for hundreds of miles over the New York wilderness and the solitudes of Canada, so far from cities, towns and settlements that if any accident befell the monoplane it would mean the end of the aviator and his companion. If perchance the long voyage through the upper air was effected in safety, who should insist the Professor was not warranted in trying the far grander one that should land him and his companion in Great Britain on their road to Africa?

Hopeless as such an attempt must be (at least until the science of aviation is much further advanced than now), it was as promising as the effort of Harvey Hamilton, to follow the flying machine by rail, steamboat, stage, and on foot or horseback. There were vast reaches over which he would have to travel by roundabout routes and at a snail's pace. Using every advantage at command, he could not get to one of the Canadian cities until at the end of several weeks.

We have no means of knowing what fancies filled the brain of the man whose powers of reasoning were warped, but who in some directions was capable of as perfect logic as is ever displayed by the most brilliant mathematician. The probable conclusion reached by him was that his pursuer would abandon the unsettled sections of the country and take a direct course to the leading Canadian seaport, with a view of heading him off on the assumption that the monoplane would meet with accident or delays on the way.

It seemed to Harvey that he had other ground—though shadowy—for hope of tracing the elusive Professor. He would not venture upon his ocean voyage, as it may be called, until satisfied that his preparations were complete. He had spoken only a short time before of his conviction that they would soon be finished. He was too skilled an aviator to start for Europe before his machine was ready. The chemical compound which he had discovered would carry him the greater part of the distance and it was reasonable to believe he needed a few days in which to perfect its composition. To effect this he would make excursions over the surrounding country, returning to his workshop to push his investigations. It followed that if this theory was correct, he would stay in the vicinity of Dawson for an indefinite though probably a brief time. If such proved the fact, Harvey had fair prospect of success by shaping his own conduct in accordance with such theory.

If I have made clear the conditions which our young friend had to face, some deception on his part will be justified. As has been said, the wording of the "Warning" posted on the door of the workshop proved that the inventor's real aim was to throw his pursuer off his track and end pursuit by him. If the Professor could be made to believe he had done this, he would use all the time necessary to complete his preparations for his stupendous aerial voyage.

These thoughts filled the brain of Harvey on his return to the Washington House in the little town of Dawson. Stepping upon the porch and seeing nothing of the landlord, he passed inside, where he came upon him seated in his big armchair, slowly puffing his briarwood.

"Will you let me know the amount of my bill?" was the guest's first greeting.

It was not necessary for the innkeeper to consult his books, and without rising from his chair he answered:

"Supper, breakfast and lodging is two dollars."

Harvey handed him the exact amount, and the landlord folded and tucked the bill into his waistcoat pocket.

"Going back to New York?" he grunted, disposed to relax now that he was about to lose a guest.

"I'm going to New Jersey where I live. I walked out to Professor Morgan's place, only to find a notice posted on the door to the effect that he had gone away for several weeks. So what's the use of my loitering about here for all that time?"

"What the Professor says you can depend on. If you come back in a fortnight, you mought git sight of him, but there's no sense in coming afore that time."

"So it would seem. Have you seen anything of him lately?"

"He hasn't been here for several days and when he does come he has powerful little to say."

Harvey did not show that he knew this reply was a falsehood. The inventor had been in the house the night before and learned of the presence of the young aviator without his machine. It remained for the latter to make him think his attempt at deception was successful. What surer method could there be than the one Harvey was following?

His next inquiry was as to the trains from the railway station at Beelsburg, a dozen miles away. The stage did not leave until early in the afternoon and generally an hour's wait was necessary before a passenger could start southward. Harvey proposed to hire a conveyance, which if it made fair progress could intercept a train that passed at noon. When the landlord named the charge for the services of such a team, the guest accepted off-hand and hurried to his room to bring down his traveling bag. He encountered daughter Ann in the hall, to whom he told his purpose. It was safer not to enlighten her as to his real intention, since nothing could be gained by doing so and she would be likely to drop some remark to her "paw" that would disclose Harvey's scheme. So with a friendly good-bye, he added to his former tip and scurried down stairs, where he had to wait only a few minutes when the open carriage drawn by a gaunt, bony horse drew up and he climbed in. The driver was a youth of about his own age, and a sort of hostler and man of all work. Harvey never met a more grouchy person. It was hard to make him say yes or no to a question, and the passenger gave it up, after letting him know he was on his way to his own home a good many miles distant.

None the less, the fellow knew his business and landed his charge at the station half an hour ahead of train time. Harvey slipped a silver half dollar into his hand and he did not so much as speak or nod, but circled around, struck his rangy animal a whack with his splintered whip and faded from sight in a cloud of dust.

Most of Harvey's time on his way home was spent in studying an elaborate map of the Adirondack region, northern New York, and the lower portion of the Dominion of Canada. His interest in this work and his retentive memory caused him to absorb knowledge rapidly and soon he began to feel more familiar with the region than he had believed possible without months of exploration.

"If I ever get through with this job I think I'll hire out as a guide for hunters in the Adirondacks. I'm told some of them are paid big wages. It's odd that Dick should be somewhere up there and it will be a good deal more odd if he and I should meet. I forget what part of the country he dated his letters from and it isn't likely he stays long in one place. Won't he be astonished if I drop down on him some fine day from the sky?"

It was on the following afternoon that Harvey Hamilton appeared again at his home near the village of Mootsport. A disappointment met him. He expected as a matter of course that his father would be in New York, but he learned that his mother and sister had accompanied him thither that morning. Harvey went to the house of Mr. Hartley, but he too was absent for the day. The caller explained everything to the wife of the farmer and she promised to transfer the information to the others that evening. To make sure on this point Harvey wrote a letter to his parents in which he told all that had occurred with him since his previous departure. He laid this missive on his fathers table in the library, said a few parting words to the servants, and then hurried out to the hangar to bring his aeroplane into service.

"I expect big things of you," he said as he carefully examined wires, ribs, engine, ailerons, propeller, rudders and every part down to the minutest detail. "It won't do to have any defect, which reminds me."

He ran to the house again and furnished himself with an outfit of the most modern fishing tackle.

"There's no saying when I may need it. If I should be lost in the Adirondack wilderness, I might have to depend upon what I can take from the lakes and streams. It won't do any harm too to add to my stock of safety matches."

There was little to make in the way of addition to his former preparations. The same bag that he had brought home was taken away swelled to plumpness by indispensable articles, while his extra coat was folded and tied to the seat, behind him, where it could not be blown away by any gale or flurry of wind. He did not think it worth while to ask for help in making a start, for the long sloping meadow was perfect for that purpose. He followed his old plan of setting the propeller revolving, when he dashed alongside the moving machine, slipped into his seat, grasped the levers and was off.

It seems incredible, even with the science of aviation so well advanced, that starting from northern New Jersey, the young aviator should reach the Adirondack region before nightfall, but such was the fact. His first stop was at Poughkeepsie where he renewed his gasoline and oil, stretched his legs, made another minute examination of his machine and answered a few of the hundreds of questions that were asked by the ever-increasing swarm of people that gathered around him. They were as friendly and good-natured as they had been to Glenn Curtiss, who made his memorable flight from Albany to New York a short time before. When Harvey soared aloft once more, he carried with him the best wishes of the cheering scores whose conduct was in pleasing contrast to that of the young farmers in eastern Pennsylvania who were bent on destroying the aeroplane and became angered enough to try to add the young aviator himself to the wreck and ruin.

CHAPTER V
BY AERIAL EXPRESS

NO more glorious panorama ever enthralled a human spectator than that upon which the eyes of Harvey Hamilton feasted while gliding northward on his way to the Adirondack region. There were towns, cities, forests, streams, and expanses of woodland in his own State of New Jersey and the white-capped Atlantic rolling to the eastward, with steamers and sailing craft dotting its surface all the way to the horizon, where the Atlantic's convexity dipped and the eye could penetrate no farther. The second greatest city in the world spread out below him, with smaller ones continually rising and sinking from view as he coursed up the Hudson valley, sometimes to the right, then to the left and again straight over the picturesque stream whose crafts of all kinds were hieing away from or to the metropolis. Absorbed as was the young aviator in the mission on which he had started he could not help gazing below and drinking in the indescribable beauty of the ever-changing picture.

"How much those who went before us lost!" he sighed; "and what delight awaits those that are coming upon the stage of life! Aviation will bring the greatest revolution mankind has ever known. It is my happy fate to be one of the pioneers. I wonder what remains before me and others. At any rate none can feel more thankful than I for the goodness of Heaven in permitting me to see this day."

As he progressed up the romantic valley after leaving Troy, his thoughts came back to the serious work before him. He had set out to save his colored friend from a dreadful fate, and to that he must bend all his energies until success or hopeless failure came.

Basing his action upon the theory that Professor Morgan had not yet started on his aerial voyage across the Atlantic, his pursuer aimed to return to the vicinity of his headquarters. It was important that he should go as near to them as he could without exposing himself to discovery. It would never do for the crazy inventor to learn that the youth's withdrawal from the field was a trick. The moment such discovery was made, that moment the last vestige of hope would be snatched from the would-be rescuer.

Harvey therefore made a circuit around Troy and Albany, and when he turned in the direction of the little country town of Dawson, became more alert than before. The local geography of the section was so impressed upon his memory that he recognized the leading points as he swept over them. Besides directing his machine, he made frequent use of his field glass. He scanned the heavens in search of the Dragon of the Skies, that he might flee from it in time. If the Professor was abroad he would not be looking for the pursuer, who counted upon detecting him first and dodging out of his sight.

When he identified Dawson in the distance he knew his supply of liquid fuel was pretty low. He could renew it at that town, but it would have been imprudent to do so, for his whole scheme would be disclosed. In an effort to avoid attracting the attention of the inhabitants, he veered to the right, sailing as near the ground as was safe. If Professor Morgan should learn that an aeroplane had been observed in the sky, his suspicions would be excited and he would see through the trick that had been played upon him.

Eight or ten miles to the northeast, in the direction of Schroon River, which empties into the lake of the same name, Harvey saw the village of Purvis, containing less than one-half the population of Dawson. Gasoline is so common an article that he was sure he could buy all he wished in that place and he shifted his course accordingly. He was still flying so low that he was not noticed until he descended in a large field a little way to the eastward. He had hardly come to rest, however, when he heard wild shouts and saw not only men and boys, but women and girls running toward him in a high state of excitement. Harvey was uneasy until he found that their curiosity did not decrease their friendliness.

"Say, Mister, can't you give a feller a ride in that gimcrack?"

The questioner was a barefooted gawky youth with big projecting front teeth. He wore a ragged straw hat, and his nankeen trousers were held up by a single leathern suspender, skewered with a nail in front. Harvey thought he might win the good-will of the crowd by gratifying the applicant and perhaps several others.

"I don't mind if you're not afraid to trust yourself with me," he replied, surveying the grinning, freckle-faced countryman.

"Gosh! what am I afeard of? If the blamed thing can carry you round the kentry, why can't it tote me, eh?"

And he laughed so hard that his shoulders bobbed up and down and the wrinkles obscured his eyes.

"All right; take your seat and hold on tight; you must sit very quiet, for if you move the least bit you may upset the machine and kill us both."

The lad, nothing abashed, climbed to his place with the help of Harvey and still grinning broadly announced that he would not so much as bat an eye while aloft.

"Let her whiz! I'm ready and I don't keer—."

At that moment a tall, muscular woman strode from the crowd, caught hold of one of the ankles of the boy above the bare foot, and jerked so hard that seemingly elongated by the energetic pull, he came bumping from his seat and struck the ground so hard that it made him grunt.

"I'll teach you how to play the fool, Josiah Bilkins! The idee! You sailing up into the sky! What are you thinkin' of yourself? Do you hear me? Take that!"

By this time Josiah had struggled to his feet, and with his hands over his ears to ward off the cuffs that were rained upon them, and amid the jeers of his acquaintances, he started on a run across the open space. But his mother was fleeter than he and kept up her castigation as they passed out of sight around the corner of a house.

None laughed harder than Harvey at the scene, and when the turmoil had subsided he said to those remaining:

"If any one would like to take a ride, I shall be glad to give it to him."

To his surprise, a middle-aged man, likewise without coat or waistcoat, wearing a dilapidated straw hat with his trousers tucked into the tops of his cowhide boots came forward. When Harvey looked into his tanned, grinning face, and noted the yellow tuft of chin whiskers, and the fast-working jaws, he recalled Uncle Tommy Waters, the weather prophet of Chesterton. Encouraging shouts were uttered by the man's friends, but they quickly ceased to allow him to talk with the visitor to their town.

"Sure the blamed thing won't kick up its heels?" asked the stoop-shouldered man, whom his neighbors called "Gin'ral."

"It never has done so."

"How fur have you kim?"

"From beyond the city of New York."

"Ye ain't lying, sonny?"

"No; do as you please about trusting or believing me."

"I'm consarned if I don't try it," remarked the General, stirred by the taunts of his neighbors. He climbed gingerly to his seat, aided by Harvey, who was much entertained by his experience thus far in Purvis. The passenger rigidly grasped a support on each side, and chewing more vigorously than before, nodded his head:

"I'm ready; let the blamed thing go!"

Cautioning him again not to shift his position while aloft, but to keep perfectly motionless, Harvey also seated himself, and asked one of the men to give the propeller a whirl. The roar and racket of the machine were deafening, but it began creeping over the grass, rapidly increasing its pace, until the moment came for the aviator to tilt the front rudder upward. At the instant the bound took place, the crowd, who were watching it all, saw the General make a dive from his seat, sprawl through the air like a frog and, lighting on his face, roll over several times before coming to a stop. The frightened Harvey made as quick a circle as he could and returned to his starting point to find the General standing among his friends, who were chaffing him for his sudden loss of courage.

"What was the matter?" asked Harvey, though he knew well enough that his passenger had yielded to a sudden panic.

"Why, I happened to think jes' as we started that I'd promised to meet Bill Smithers at his home and it wouldn't do fur me to make him wait, so I jumped."

"I was here all the time a-lookin' at you," replied the sarcastic Smithers.

"That's so," said the unabashed General, "but I didn't know it till I observed you."

"What did you want to see me fur, Gin'ral?"

"To git you to pay me that two dollars you borrered t'other day."

Smithers joined in the laugh at his expense and Harvey inquired whether any one else wished to take a ride with him. But the panic of the only passenger at liberty to accept the invitation seemed to have its effect upon the others, and no one went forward.

Harvey now engaged one of the bystanders to bring him a supply of oil and gasoline and filled his tank. Then he bade his new friends good-bye and sailed away.

His plan was to go as near as was safe to the shop of Professor Morgan, then descend, leave his aeroplane and make his further investigations on foot. He could do this so guardedly that there was little danger of detection. To attempt it with his machine would bring certain discovery.

As before, he rose only high enough to clear the large trees, many of which were taller than any of the buildings. The surrounding country was wooded and mountainous. To the northward he made out two peaks with a hazy ridge in the horizon and knew that many miles of craggy wilderness stretched beyond. He was all nerves while drawing near the workshop, a half mile to the north of Dawson, for necessity drove him forward fast and the danger of detection increased with every hundred yards he advanced.

Convinced that he had gone as far as was prudent he sought out a suitable landing place, fixing upon what had once been a cultivated field of several acres, but was now lush grass, inclosed on all sides by woods and matted undergrowth. As nearly as he could tell he was within less than a mile of the building from which all trespassers had been warned under peril of death. He had no time now to give to anything except the work of landing and he did that with a skill that would have won the praise of Professor Sperbeck, his old instructor in the difficult science of aeronautics, could he have seen it.

As soon as the wheels stopped running over the ground, Harvey stepped out and pushed the aeroplane to the side of the meadow and as near the forest as possible. He even shoved it a little way into the brush and under the limbs of the trees, taking care to injure none of its parts. The reason for this precaution he explained to himself:

"Professor Morgan has the eye of a hawk, and if I leave the machine in the open, he will catch sight of it if he passes within a mile. He will hardly see it, now that it is so well screened."

There was risk of another nature in all this, but he could think of no way to avoid it. If the weather should turn bad, the apparatus was not well protected. He would have given a good deal for the verdict of Uncle Tommy Waters, but made himself believe that no change of the character feared was likely to occur.

If any persons had observed the descent, they might make their way to the spot and wreck the machine or disable it through their curiosity, but he had to take the chances in that respect also, and since there was no choice he did not hesitate. He had located the shop of the Professor so clearly while in the air that he was in no doubt as to the course to take. He saw no signs of a path or trail, and travel was as rough as that encountered on his former visit.

Standing on the edge of the rocky forest, the young aviator raised his field glasses and began a study of the visible heavens, and within five minutes of doing so he made a startling discovery.

Far in the northern sky he descried an object that looked like a stupendous eagle, soaring through the air on its way southward. It was traveling fast and steadily increased in size. Careful scrutiny left no doubt that it was an aerocar, and a second look revealed that it was a monoplane!

"It is the Professor!" exclaimed Harvey, keeping the binoculars in place. "How fortunate that I hid my machine when I did! He doesn't dream that I'm within hundreds of miles of him."

The course of the car was toward the spot where the mysterious cabin stood in the woods. All doubt that the air man was going thither was removed. Harvey's theory was verified. The crazy inventor was not yet ready to start on his momentous voyage and was experimenting before doing so. Now that he had driven his pursuer off the scent as he believed, he could complete his investigations in his own shop where no one dared disturb him.

As the monoplane coursed swiftly through the air, a faint fear that it might not be the Dragon of the Skies caused Harvey to listen intently. Had the machine been of the ordinary kind he would have heard its racket some minutes before, but his straining senses caught no sound.

"It's the Professor and no mistake; I can see his erect body in his seat and almost recognize those long, grizzled whiskers."

But now when the monoplane had come still nearer, Harvey Hamilton made the alarming discovery that the crank inventor was alone in his flying ship.

Where was Bohunkus Johnson?

CHAPTER VI
RECONNOITERING

THE all-important question still confronted the young aviator: where was his colored friend, Bohunkus Johnson?

There might be several answers to the query, but none was satisfactory. Possibly he was at the workshop of Professor Morgan, or had been set down at the end of the experimental tours the inventor was making, or the fate which Harvey dreaded may have already overtaken him.

"The one thing for me to do is to have another look at the Professor's place at close range, when he has no thought of my being near. I shall surely be able to learn something worth while."

Our friend kept the Dragon of the Skies under scrutiny so long as it remained in his field of vision. It was heading toward the cabin and in a brief while dipped from sight. The inventor had descended to resume work.

The day was drawing to a close. The sun had set, and twilight was creeping over the dismal wilderness. It was a hard walk through the broken, rocky solitude where he could not find any trail but simply knew the right course to follow. He had brought a goodly package of sandwiches with him and he now ate of the lunch. Fully a dozen remained in the paper bag that was placed on the seat before the tank, reserved to serve him on the morrow. He was loath to leave the aeroplane unwatched, but, as has been shown, there was no help for it, and he now trusted to the good fortune that had clung so markedly to him from the time he first left home.

With a final inspection of the machine, he skirted the edge of the wood to the farther corner and then went toward the inventor's headquarters. It was hard work from the first. He was forced to go around huge boulders and masses of rock, push through the intricate undergrowth, now and then checked and driven to make long detours, but he kept the right course and knew he had only to persevere to reach the spot in the end. The moon did not rise until late, but the sky was clear, and studded with brilliant stars, while the partial lighting up of the obscurity enabled him to avoid going astray.

As nearly as he could judge he had traversed half the distance when, without thought of any such thing, he came abruptly to the margin of a large pond or lake. He could not recall having noticed a sheet of water in studying his map of the region and was in a dilemma. In the obscurity the gleaming surface stretched beyond his vision on the right and left, nor could he see anything but darkness in front.

"I must cross in some way," he reflected, "but how shall I do it? I shouldn't mind taking a long swim, but it would be awkward in my clothes and I shouldn't like to call upon the Professor in the costume of Adam and Eve."

He had not left any of his garments with the aeroplane, for there was no saying when he was likely to need his outer coat. While the temperature was mild, a certain crispness natural to the season brooded in the air, and when he thrust his hand into the water he found it thrillingly cold. He inclined to the plan of fastening enough dry limbs together to float his garments, while he swam and pushed the little raft in front. He would not have hesitated to do this despite the chilliness of the water, could he have been certain that the swim would not prove a long one.

True, he was within a half mile of the cabin, as he figured it, and it would seem that slight risk was involved.

"There's no saying how far I should have to tramp to go round the lake," he said, as he turned the question over in his mind, "but the other shore can't be very distant. The swim will do me good and I'll take it."

He began groping along the shore in quest of the material with which to make the float. It was while he was doing this that he uttered an exclamation of delight over another unexpected piece of good fortune. He almost fell over the prow of a canoe drawn lightly up the bank where its owner had left it. The graceful craft was a dozen feet long and the broad-bladed paddle lay in the bottom ready for use whenever needed.

"If that isn't rare luck then there was never such a thing," added Harvey after examining the primitive boat, which, Indian fashion, was constructed of birch bark sewed and gummed together and thoroughly water-tight. He knew something of canoes, shells and motor boats and had no misgiving of his ability to handle this craft.

But what of the owner? Where was he and when was he likely to return? Suppose he was a hunter or woodman who would discover him before he could get far from shore? What treatment would he deal out to the one that was running off with his property?

Hoping that the man might be near and could be hired to set him on the other side, Harvey called "Hello!" three or four times, in a voice that carried several hundred yards. There was no reply however, a fact which convinced him that even if the owner soon returned the one who was making use of his property would be beyond rifle range.

Night was advancing and Harvey did not linger. He laid his outer coat in the farther end, and stepping carefully into the unstable structure, picked up the paddle, and pressing it against the bank, pushed the canoe well out upon the placid bosom of the lake. Taking his bearings, he glanced often at the sky and with the aid of the constellation Ursa Major (which always seemed to confront him when he looked into the sky), he proceeded as truly as if steering by compass. The paddle was light, with a broad blade at one end. Facing the way he was going, he dipped it first on the right and then the left, so gently that he caused only a faint ripple and made no noise.

He smiled at the discovery which came within the following five minutes. The wooded shore in front loomed to sight at the same time with the terminus of the lake on his right. A detour of two hundred yards would have led him around the body of water, and a swim for the same distance would have landed him on the shore opposite his starting point.

"I hope the owner won't feel offended when he finds his canoe has been shifted to another point, for he won't have to travel far to get it again."

A few minutes later, Harvey drew the boat up the bank and resumed his journey toward the workshop of Professor Morgan. It will be remembered that he was now quite near the little town of Dawson, which he left to the right. He held to his bearings so well that he came directly upon the place where the trail turned off from the highway and began picking his course to the cabin.

He was now "skating on thin ice." The inventor might be going to the Washington House for his evening meal, or possibly returning therefrom. In either case, the utmost caution was necessary to avert a meeting with him. The trail over which

Harvey was advancing with the utmost care may be described as an alley or avenue or cañon, walled in for most of the way by rocks and overhanging trees, with open places at intervals, where the star-gleam showed objects indistinctly for a hundred feet or less.

It will be noted that the youth had to guard the front and rear, for there was no saying from which direction danger would appear. He remembered the character of the path, and stepped as softly as a burglar stealing over a carpeted floor. When he had gone a few paces, he paused, listened, and peered into the inclosing gloom. He had little fear of meeting strangers, for the Professor had impressed all with the peril they ran in yielding to their curiosity. It was the fanatical inventor whom he held in dread.

But his tense senses told nothing, and Harvey finally turned the corner of the rocky avenue, where there was a small open space, and the cabin loomed before him. He stood staring, wondering and speculating as to what it all could mean. The building was utterly dark and silent. Its shadowy outlines showed against the starlit sky, but it was as if he were looking upon some huge tomb. The gloom would not permit him to see whether the Dragon of the Skies was resting in the hangar provided for it, but he believed the strange air craft was there, awaiting the whim of its owner.

While making his guarded survey, Harvey did not forget the delicate situation in which he stood. He was partially veiled in shadow and though he heard not the slightest sound he turned his head and looked back over the trail which he had followed to the spot. A few rods distant it showed a slight rise, so that he came down a moderate slope to where he had halted. This low elevation threw the summit of the incline against the starlit sky behind it and at the moment of looking, Harvey saw Professor Morgan's gaunt form in silhouette striding over the rise and coming toward him, with the well-known linen duster flapping about his heels.

The watcher slipped a little farther to one side, where he was effectively screened, and silently awaited the man whose soft footfalls could now be heard. A minute later he passed so near to where the eavesdropper stood that a step toward him would have enabled Harvey to touch him with outstretched hand. But the last thing of which the Professor was thinking was of intruders into his domain. The tall form stalked across the brief open space, halted an instant in front of the door, at which the inventor fumbled a moment and then passed inside.

Almost immediately the interior was flooded with dazzling light, brighter and more vivid than that of the noonday sun. Through the plate glass window could be seen the endless paraphernalia of the workshop of an inventive genius—the lathe, bottles of chemicals, boxes, tools, coils of wire, retorts, queer-shaped utensils, some suspended on the wall, others resting on shelves, and many as partially revealed lying on the solid planking of the floor. The Professor himself took a few steps toward the rear of his shop and thus came into full view. He did not doff his headgear nor remove the linen duster which hung almost to his ankles. Harvey saw him reach up to one of the hooks on the wall, lift off a coil of copper wire, and then bending over the lathe, set a small wheel revolving rapidly by means of the treadle which one of his feet pressed. No one could guess the nature of what he was doing, except that it was a part of his experimentation for the perfecting of the monoplane which was already a wonder of its kind.

What Harvey Hamilton looked upon was of absorbing interest, but he could not forget the painful fact that Bohunkus Johnson was nowhere in sight, and the painful question which he had asked himself so many times still remained unanswered. It was certain the colored youth was not here.

For a half hour the spectator stood as motionless as a graven image, staring, listening, wondering what was coming next. The inventor now and then moved about the brilliantly lighted room, but he was busy as a bee and as absorbed in his work as if only a few minutes remained at his command in which to complete the most important task of his life. By and by he lighted a briarwood pipe, and never once removed it from his mouth. The clearness of Harvey's view was proved by the sight of each little puff of smoke which at intervals shot along the stem from his lips.

Being assured that Bunk was nowhere near the place, Harvey saw nothing to be gained by acting further as eavesdropper. He was withdrawing, when, as suddenly as it had been lighted, the workshop was shrouded in darkness. He waited awhile thinking some slight accident had occurred, but the impenetrable gloom continued. Professor Morgan evidently was through his work for the night, though it would be supposed that like most monomaniacs he would have been unconscious of the passage of time.

"It may mean he has solved the problem over which he has studied so long," thought Harvey, softly groping his way back to the trail, along which he threaded his course to the highroad and then as nearly as he could judge to the point where he entered it when coming from the small lake. He was in a more confused state of mind than ever, and could not decide what step he should next take.

He had settled upon one thing: while so near Dawson he must so far as possible keep out of sight of everybody. He dared not go to the hotel for lodging and it was imprudent to apply at any private house. His plan was to return to where he had left the aeroplane, wrap himself in his outer coat and cuddle up in the seat for the remainder of the night. The weather was so comparatively mild that the exposure would not harm him nor need he be uncomfortable. There is something attractive to a robust, rugged youth in the idea of camping out or roughing it, besides which he was uneasy over leaving his machine without guard. He was in a section quite well settled and the finding of the canoe showed that people were liable to pass that way at any time.

Having now no trail to follow, Harvey could not accurately retrace his steps, but held to the course so well that he reached the shore of the lake at the time expected. But nothing was to be seen of the canoe that had brought him over. He made a brief but unsuccessful search.

"It can't be far off," was his conclusion; "the owner will have no trouble in finding it, if he hasn't already done so and gone back to the other side."

Recalling the slight expanse of water, Harvey picked his way along the margin until he reached the curving end, around which he passed, and then resumed his direct course to the clearing on whose edge he had left his machine. He saw and heard nothing to disturb him during his return and reached the spot while the night was still comparatively young.

CHAPTER VII
AN UNWELCOME VISITOR

YIELDING to a feeling of slight uneasiness, Harvey Hamilton lighted several matches and made an inspection of his aeroplane. With vast relief he found it unharmed. If any one had come upon the machine he had not molested it. It was ready for service and he had a good supply of gasoline and oil.

He had placed his bag of sandwiches on the rear seat. Removing the food to the one he used when sailing through the air, he adjusted himself in the upper seat. Here with his coat wrapped about him he said his prayers, and settled down for a night's slumber. He was tired and needed rest, but his mind was so full of what he had learned, and with speculations as to the immediate future, that he remained awake far longer than was his usual habit.

A strange theory took shape in his mind. It was in effect that when Professor Morgan made his first experimental flight he took Bohunkus with him to some point where he had been left with orders to stay until his master — as the man undoubtedly was — called for him. If he kept Bunk at the "works," the boy was quite sure to meet others who might persuade him to run away. Hidden somewhere in the wilds of the Adirondacks he would not dare do this, but would meekly obey instructions. He would be kept there until the Professor had perfected his invention and returned, when he would pick up the youth and start on their trip to Africa. The question of food was simple: Morgan could readily take what the fellow needed, though not all he wished, to him.

On the supposition that our young friend was right in his surmises, what could he do to save his comrade? In what respect was the situation improved or the problem simplified? A man can disguise his personal appearance and often successfully shadow another, so long as both keep their feet on the solid earth. But nothing of that nature was possible in the present instance. The first sight which Professor Morgan should catch of Harvey's biplane would tell the whole story. He would know the youth had returned to the lower Adirondacks to take Bohunkus Johnson from him. The discovery could not fail to throw him into a flaming rage, and he would exert himself to destroy the audacious pursuer. Harvey felicitated himself upon his possession of the revolver and a supply of cartridges. While he did not hold the crazy inventor in fear, he dreaded unspeakably a hostile encounter with him, for the consequences were sure to be tragical.

Finally the wearied youth drifted into dreamland, slightly chilled but on the whole fairly comfortable. He became cramped and as a consequence awoke before the night had fully passed. He shifted his posture and noticed that the risen moon lighted the plain and showed the dark line of the forest on the farther side. He had reached the point of half consciousness, with his nerves at the highest tension, when he was startled by hearing a footfall among the shadows at his side.

"Somebody is prowling near," was his thought as he sat upright and listened. He heard again the sound of rustling leaves, which showed he was not mistaken.

"Hello out there!" he called in a guarded undertone; "who are you?"

The noise ceased and there was no reply. Once more the rustling was noticeable.

"Why don't you answer me? What do you want?—Great heavens!"

Well might he utter the exclamation, for there was an ominous growl and a big black body lumbered from the wood in the moonlight and swung toward the aeroplane.

"A bear, as sure as I live!" gasped Harvey, leaving his seat at a bound and taking care to land opposite the intruder. The latter stopped, looked at him and rearing on its hind legs, reached out one of its huge paws and drew the bag of sandwiches from its place. He must have scented the meat between the slices of bread.

The food dropped to the ground and he clawed the paper into strips, thrusting his snout among the tidbits, which he began devouring with the gusto of Bohunkus Johnson himself. No doubt he found them delicious, but the drawback was that the supply only whetted his appetite for more and there was none to be had. Again he rose on his hind feet and began exploring the framework of the machine.

"Confound you!" shouted the alarmed Harvey; "you'll smash things all to pieces!"

It looked the next moment as if the bear meant to climb into the seat and take charge of matters. The grim humor of the situation struck the boy.

"I wonder if he has had lessons in aviation and wants to show off his skill. Wouldn't he cut a fine figure in my place, yanking the levers and cruising round in the sky? What would Professor Morgan think if he saw him? Probably he would suspect it was I trying to disguise myself."

But there was a serious side to the situation. The machine was likely to be injured beyond the present power of repair unless the brute were driven away. After nosing for some minutes he seemed to know that no more sandwiches remained. That being the case, what more tempting morsel could he ask than a plump American youngster about seventeen years old? Probably from his standpoint there was none, for at this juncture he dropped back on all fours and started round the aeroplane with a view of sampling that youngster.

"This is a good time for me to leave," was the hasty conclusion of Harvey, who plunged into the woods, with the bear in hot pursuit. He knew something of such animals, and although he could see only dimly in the gloom under the trees, he recognized a sapling by running against it and nearly knocking himself senseless. He staggered back, recovered himself, and grasping the small trunk, ascended it faster than he had ever before climbed a tree. He strove desperately, expecting every second that the enormous claws of the bear would grip one of his legs and drag him back to the ground, but when he had gone so high that his support began bending over alarmingly, he knew he was secure for the time.

A few moonbeams straggled through the limbs and showed the dim outlines of the shaggy brute, which once more rose on his rear legs and reached upward, as if he expected his supper to drop into his maws.

"You can wait there till doomsday, but you won't see me coming down to meet you."

Harvey was twelve or fifteen feet from the ground, enough to ensure his safety so long as present conditions continued. He had reached a limb half as thick as the sapling and he swung a leg over it. Thus he was able to sustain himself, but the position soon began to be irksome. The limb chafed his leg, and when he shifted it as much as he could the relief lasted only a few minutes.

Meanwhile, he kept his enemy under observation. The ursus species is not noted for its intelligence, but after awhile this one decided he was baffled for the time. His kind cannot climb a small tree, though they find little difficulty in going up a shaggy trunk around which their claws do not meet. This specimen sank back on all fours, but held his place at the foot of the sapling.

"Now what is he thinking about?" Harvey asked himself, with a chill of fear the next minute, when his support was violently shaken; "I wonder whether he's going to pull up this young tree by the roots. I don't believe he can do it, but if he knew enough he could wrap his paws around it and draw it over to bring me within reach."

The shaking ceased, as if the bear had given up that idea, if indeed he had ever held it. The obscurity was too deep for Harvey to make sure, but he fancied that a tree, probably an oak, with trunk several feet in diameter, grew so near the sapling that it was within reach of his hand.

"Like enough he will climb it," reflected Harvey, "till he is higher than I am and then drop down on my head. Why don't he give up and clear out?"

A little later it looked as if the brute had decided to do the very thing a certain youth up a tree wished him to do. He lumbered off a few paces, taking him beyond sight in the dense shadows. The rustling of the leaves grew fainter, and by and by ceased altogether. Harvey's hopes rose, when fifteen minutes passed without the sound of a growl or the stirring of the dead leaves on the ground.

"I believe he has gone," whispered the lad, as if afraid his voice might bring back his enemy. "But it's best to make sure."

By and by the chafing by the limb which he bestrode grew unbearable. He drew his leg over and began sliding down the smooth trunk, inching along, often pausing, listening, and peering into the dusk, ready to scramble up again on the first sign from his foe.

After a long time, he felt the toe of one shoe softly touch the leaves. He lowered the other and stood erect. The relief from his onerous posture was great.

"It does a fellow good," he mused, "I wonder how those hunters stand it when they are treed and kept off the ground for hours at a time. I'm glad I'm rid of this plaguy bear—Great Cæsar!"

A terrific threshing of the undergrowth showed that the brute was returning like a cyclone. He had gone only a few paces, as if to tempt the fugitive to do the very thing he had done. I have said that Harvey Hamilton when first chased by the black bear climbed the sapling more quickly than he had ever done a similar thing before. I must add that this second exhibition in that line surpassed his first, and established a record. In a twinkling he was up on his perch again, with one of his muscular legs doubled over the limb, feeling as if he would stay there a week before running so fearful a risk as the one from which he had just escaped.

"Of all creatures in the world," he said disgustedly, "the bear is the meanest. I never harmed this one, and what has he got against me? He stole my lunch and wants to use me as dessert.

It isn't very pleasant up here," he sighed, "but it beats being chewed up by a bear. I wonder whether there's anybody near enough to hear me if I yell."

He was reluctant to resort to this, since the coming of any person in the circumstances was likely to interfere with his search for his missing comrade. He decided to wait, hoping that after all the bear would grow tired of hanging around and swing off into the woods.

Harvey held on like a hero, shifting his position so far as he was able, until it became so irksome that he decided to slide down the trunk and run for another tree. His dread was that in making the attempt he would blunder and not find the refuge at instant command; for with a ravenous bear at one's heels no person can afford to move leisurely.

When it seemed that an hour had passed, though the time was much less, he called out, pretended to descend the sapling and really did go part way. The silence was so complete that hope sprang up again, and by and by he glided slowly down inch by inch until his feet once more touched the leaves. He stood waiting and listening, but heard nothing to send him scrambling back to his perch.

"I'll try it!" he said and began stealing toward the edge of the wood where the aeroplane was half hidden in the foliage and under the limbs of the trees. He stepped as carefully as an Indian scout, with hands outstretched, feeling his way and ready to climb in a flash another trunk the instant it became necessary. He knew he was advancing so silently that if the brute was within two or three yards he could not hear him.

Harvey took comfort in the thought that whatever might happen, he was through with the refuge that had tried him so sorely. There couldn't be another precisely like it and that of itself was immeasurable relief.

"I should prefer a big tree even with the risk of his following me—Confound it!"

Just then he caught his foot in a thick root which lay parallel to his course and with the free end projecting toward him. He raised his shoe to step over it, but the obstruction rose also, and despite a fierce effort to save himself he fell forward on his hands and knees with a racket that could have been heard far away in the stillness. Certain that his foe would be upon him the next moment, he made a dash in the dim light, but was brought up standing by an obtruding limb which slipped under his chin and fairly lifted him clear of the ground. For a single second, he fancied his head had been shorn off his shoulders, and he made a wild dash for another sapling. He collided with a trunk and in his panic turned again, and then suddenly halted.

Surely, if the bear was anywhere near, he would rush for the spot, but he heard nothing. He now changed his course so as to reach the open within a few yards of his aeroplane. Most likely the brute had grown tired of waiting and gone off. The youth might have left his sapling some time before and escaped all he had suffered.

CHAPTER VIII
THE PROFESSOR LEADS THE WAY

HARVEY HAMILTON was making his way toward the aeroplane, when his right hand touched a big lump at his hip. Reaching down to learn what it was, he drew forth his six-shooter.

"Well, I'll be hanged! I'm the champion idiot of the twentieth century!" he exclaimed, with a pang of self-disgust as he looked at the small weapon. "Every chamber is loaded, and I have a lot of cartridges in my pocket, but I forgot all about them until this minute! While I was chafing my legs on that limb I might have filled the bear with lead. His snout wasn't a dozen feet from me, and though I didn't see clearly I couldn't have missed him if I had tried."

He certainly had cause for exasperation. While a Colt's revolver isn't a very formidable weapon, and hunters as a rule do not seek big game with small arms, yet the modern make possesses great penetrative powers and it is quite likely that, counting Harvey's reserve ammunition, he might have given the bear his quietus. Strange that our young friend never realized he was armed until the necessity for it had passed.

"I wish he would show up again," he added, peering around in the gloom; "I should like to square matters with him for what he made me go through."

But the brute was not seen or heard again, and perhaps it was as well for the young aviator, who might have been disappointed in the effectiveness of his weapon.

A pleasing fact became manifest. Night was ended and moonlight was giving place to the increasing glow in the eastern sky that showed day was breaking. The hours of trouble, annoyance, vexation and danger were over and he must gather up the threads of life again. He was hungry, but no food was within immediate reach, and he could afford to wait until the situation cleared before seeking nourishment. He was within easy reach of thriving settlements, towns, and even cities of considerable size. To the north stretched the picturesque Adirondacks, with their wealth of streams, rivers and lakes, their vast areas of wilderness and many recesses where only the solitary hunter had as yet forced his way. Hundreds of people in quest of health and recreation were roaming through the wilds, living in log cabins or tents, or sleeping in blankets by wood fires, kindled in the depth of the solitude. They spent the glorious days in fishing, tramping and breathing the life-giving ozone, which sent them back to their duties invigorated, strengthened and renewed in body and spirit. It was a famous clergyman who, a half century before, published a book of his experiences in the Adirondacks, insisting that the mountains would cure men who had almost reached the last stages of consumption. The tonic properties of the region are extraordinary and the entrancing story sent droves thither. The majority were disappointed by his glowing pictures and when they emerged and registered their names at the primitive hotels on the outskirts, they added, "Murray's Fools." None the less, unnumbered invalids have found the section a veritable land of hope.

There was no thought of anything of this nature in the mind of Harvey Hamilton when he stood beside his aeroplane, after an inspection had shown him it was in perfect condition and ready for whatever service he required of it. As is often the case with the brain which is perplexed at night, it was clarified in the morning. He was confronted by a formidable task, but his policy was settled.

He fully believed that Professor Morgan after studying his invention in his workshop, subjected it to the decisive test in the open air, by sailing well to the northward and returning to his retreat when he discovered any defect. The distance passed might be ten, fifteen, twenty or a greater number of miles. He had not yet perfected his invention, but expected to do so quite soon. He was resolute in his purpose to carry Bohunkus Johnson across the ocean to Africa, and would fight to prevent any one taking the negro from him. With the whimsical persistence of an unbalanced brain he grew to distrust Bunk himself. The dusky youth had asked that he might be a passenger on the wonderful journey, and having received permission, would be held to the agreement.

It was this state of mind that led the inventor to transport his assistant, as he may be considered, to the northern terminus of those experimental flights, and there leave him until the time should come to start on the aerial voyage to the other side of the world. As has been said, it was an easy matter to take such food as he required, and Bohunkus having no weapons and being in the heart of an unknown wilderness, would be terrified by the thought of trying to make his way out without some one to guide him.

Such in brief was the theory that Harvey had formed and upon which he decided to work until its error appeared. As he figured matters, the great problem to solve was the location of the spot where Bohunkus was held a virtual prisoner, for the young aviator put from him the fear that the crazy Professor had made way with Bunk.

If Harvey was right in his surmises, the monoplane would soon wing its way northward, passing not far from the spot where the other machine was partially hidden on the edge of the small meadow. Harvey must learn so far as he could where the Professor's destination lay. It would be easy to do this, provided he could pursue without danger of discovery, but that was impossible: some other method must be followed.

Harvey decided to wait where he was until the monoplane sailed past and then watch its course through his field glass. If he failed to locate the precise spot, he would approximate it and narrow the area of search.

The aeroplane rested on the northern side of the clearing, from which position it was impossible, because of the intervening trees, to see the country lying in that direction. It was so early in the morning that Harvey felt safe in walking to the other side, where his observation would be clear. Prudence suggested that he should not expose himself to the risk of detection, and it would have been easy to skirt the open, thus keeping out of sight for the whole distance, but the danger was seemingly so slight, that he did not hesitate to move out from the margin of the wood toward the opposite limit of the unfenced meadow.

Straightway he received a lesson which he could never forget and which came within a hair of upsetting all his carefully laid plans. He was in the middle of the space when there was a whirring rush overhead as of the wings of a mighty bird, and Professor Morgan in his monoplane shot past directly above the youth, at a height of not more than two hundred feet. Harvey stood still, dumfounded and scared, for he was sure he was or would be discovered in the next instant. Staring upward, he saw the well-remembered machine and read the ominous name painted on the under side of the immense wings: "The Dragon of the Skies." The gaunt, long-limbed Professor sat upright, staring ahead with his hands grasping the levers, while he watched every movement of his car. So absorbed was he in this task that he did not glance downward at the form standing like a statue and gazing up at him.

It was the narrowest escape conceivable for Harvey Hamilton. He waited until the monoplane in its arrowy flight was several hundred yards away, and still going with the speed of the wind. Even then if the Professor should look behind him, he could not fail to see the spectator on the ground. In a panic, the latter broke into a run, not pausing until under the shadow of the protecting limbs of the trees. There he waited, glass in hand, and raised it to his eyes when the gigantic bird was a long way off.

"He did not wait for breakfast," was the conclusion of Harvey; "which may mean that he intends soon to return, or will eat his morning meal somewhere else, or will go without it altogether."

The sky was as clear and radiant as before, and stepping into the open, the young aviator leveled his binoculars at the inventor and his machine. They seemed to be aiming for the mountainous ridge ten or twelve miles away.

"If he stops on this side," thought Harry, "it will mean that Bunk is there awaiting him; if he goes over the summit, it will signify that beyond it is the place."

For the twentieth time, the youth blessed the makers of the admirable field glass which adds so markedly to the power of the natural eye. The whole expanse of romantic country, with its masses of rocks, belts of forest, wild, uncultivated land, broad fields, small, winding streams, scattered dwellings, three villages at varying distances, rough surface of hill, valley and precipitous elevations, some of which deserved the name of mountains, was spread before him. The ridge, like a mighty wall, shut in this impressive prospect on the north. The side of the ridge was covered with a growth of exuberant though somewhat stunted trees, gray towering masses of rocks showing at intervals; a couple of tumbling waterfalls, whose bases looked like rumpled snow, could also be seen.

Harvey Hamilton, however, had no eye for any of these: his interest lay in that object which was coursing through space at tremendous speed, as if it meant to dive into the forest which blocked its course. He kept gently shifting the focal distance of the glasses so as to hold the monoplane in distinct view, though the edges of the wings showed at times a fringe of prismatic hues that did not interfere, however, with his vision.

Professor Morgan was flying low, but at the base of the ridge, when Harvey expected to see him make a landing, he used his elevating rudder and skimmed upward toward the summit. The picture was that of an enormous bird which with its vast wings outspread was scaling the mountainside by stepping lightly on the treetops and lofty rocks. Up, up, he climbed with dizzying swiftness, was silhouetted for a moment against the clear sky, and then shot out of the watcher's field of vision.

"Bohunkus is on the other side," was Harvey's conclusion, as he screwed up the glasses and shut them in their leathern case, which he slipped over his shoulder.

It was guesswork as to when the Professor would come back. He might make a brief circuit in the sky beyond and return in a few minutes to his workshop, or be out of sight for hours. It might occur to him that it was wise to eat breakfast and to get food for his dusky assistant. Be all this as it may, Harvey decided to act at once, since nothing was to be gained otherwise.

He ran across the open to his machine, pulled it clear of the undergrowth and limbs, pointed it toward the western limit of the clearing, spun the propeller round, and sprang into his accustomed seat in time to direct the fast rising speed. He had a good supply of fuel and the biplane worked smoothly. Swerving to the north, he "put on steam" and was off.

His plan was to spin ahead until he reached the base of the ridge, or perhaps passed a part of the way up its side. He would be on the watch for a good landing place, hide the aeroplane as before, and then press his investigations on foot.

Before he had gone half the distance, he abandoned the plan of flying part way up the ridge. A dread of the Professor's return grew, and his eyes began roaming over the surface in quest of a safe place to descend. He regretted having come thus far, and resolved to take the first chance that offered. It appeared on a slight swell near the base of the ridge, but somewhat to the right of the course he was following. It was not the spot he would have selected had he not been pressed for time, but such as it was he had to accept it and he believed it would answer.

He was not in a settled section, though one of the villages could not have been more than two miles to the eastward. The ground upon which he rested his hopes could not have contained more than a couple of acres and the upper end was shut in by a lot of boulders which threatened to play havoc with his machine. Both on the left and right, however, were undergrowth and stunted pines that promised to be a good hiding place for the aeroplane. Accordingly, he dropped as low as was safe, shut off his motor and dipped to the rough ground. He landed with a bump that came near unseating him, and would have shattered his front rudder against the boulders had he not managed to veer his course so as to avoid them in time.

"I don't fancy this business," he muttered, as he stepped to the ground and looked the machine over; "the folks at Garden City know how to construct these things, for this one has stood a good deal of jarring without harm so far as I can see."

It was a work of considerable difficulty to work the biplane among the trees where it was not likely to be seen by any one passing overhead, though in plain sight of a person on the ground. Some five or six hundred feet had to be climbed to reach the summit. The surface was of the roughest character, his way leading around piles of stone, through thick woods, which fortunately were not cluttered with undergrowth, across deep gullies, and so steep in some places that it was trying even to a professional guide or hunter.

Standing thus and debating the situation, Harvey caught the murmur of the waterfall on his right. He recalled that it was near, and would have paid it a visit had not more important matters demanded attention.

CHAPTER IX
MEETING AN OLD FRIEND

IT was a half hour's climb to the top of the ridge, it being so precipitous in places that even a lusty youth like Harvey Hamilton had to pause more than once to rest his limbs and regain his wind. He accomplished his task in due time and reaching the crest, uttered an exclamation of amazement at the wonderful beauty of the landscape spread before him.

He had crossed the boundary of the county and was in Essex, which includes nearly all of the romantic Adirondack region, familiar to the thousands who visit it every year. As far as the vision could travel were wooded mountain peaks, craggy spurs, lakes, some of considerable size, the headwaters of the Hudson and other rivers, waterfalls, dashing streams, the country dotted here and there with straggling hamlets, a fashionable hotel or two, scattered cabins and rude dwellings, while tiny columns of smoke climbing through the treetops told where parties had their camps and were living in the open, with the sensible resolve to get all that the forest, redolent with spruce and balsam, could give them.

With the aid of his glass, Harvey identified a canoe containing a man and woman, the latter paddling up the winding stream far to the left, while on the shore of the lake, to the right, gleamed the white tent of some campers. He even recognized the tiny figures moving about, and saw a man enter a canoe and hurry out upon the sheet of water, which gleamed like a vast mirror of silver.

The view was worth traveling thousands of miles to enjoy. In all his wanderings through Switzerland, the Tyrol, and Italy, Harvey had beheld nothing like it. While those parts of the Old World far surpass the Adirondacks in magnificence and grandeur, there was a certain witching charm in this place not easily describable that enthralled the young American and held him mute under a spell that no European scene had been able to weave about him.

While in other circumstances he could have stood or sat for hours drinking in the fascinating beauty, he could not keep his thoughts from the serious task upon which he had entered days before. Bohunkus Johnson, if alive, was in peril from the demented man who held him a prisoner, and his rescue must be accomplished without waste of time.

Somewhere in that unrivaled landscape, Professor Morgan had gone with his monoplane. Possibly he had crossed the limit of the searcher's vision, but the latter did not think it likely. At any rate he determined to examine the territory at his feet before entering new fields.

The prosaic truth forced itself upon Harvey Hamilton that his most pressing need just then was food. He was sure he never felt quite so hungry, and there was no call for him to suffer so long as he was in a land of plenty, where hospitality is the law.

His first intention was to go down the slope to the lake, on whose bank the tent stood. He knew he would be welcome and be given abundantly of what he needed. But the spot was two miles off at least, and somehow he disliked meeting a party of jovial campers, as they were likely to be. He was not in the mood for jest and quip and feared that the contact would not help him in his self-appointed task.

In the opposite direction from the lake, nestling in a small clearing, was a cabin similar to those which he had seen during his adventurous days in eastern Pennsylvania. It was not more than a third as far from where he stood as the camp. While he observed no one moving about, a tiny spiral of smoke climbing from the stone chimney showed that the dwelling had occupants. He decided to go thither.

This compelled him to leave his aeroplane behind. Had the distance been greater he would have used it, though still dreading a sudden return of the crazy inventor and his machine. His own brief flight to the spot did not seem to have attracted attention and he gave the matter no further thought, but set out at once.

As he drew near the humble structure he was favorably impressed. It was made of logs, but the two or three acres of surrounding ground were under cultivation and the vegetables were not only plentiful and vigorous, but there was an air of neatness brooding over all, that proved the owner and occupant to be thrifty and tasteful. The front of the house was covered with climbing vines and flowers, and the windowpanes were clean, as was the little porch upon which he stepped.

That which he now saw pleased him still more, for an old-fashioned latchstring hung outside in accord with the primitive form of welcome. When the leathern string thus shows it says: "Come in without knocking."

All the same, Harvey hardly felt warranted in accepting the invitation. Instead, he knocked sharply, and straightway bumped into another surprise. He heard quick footsteps, the lifting of the latch from within, and then the door was drawn back. He had raised his hat in salutation but recoiled in pleased astonishment.

"Well, I declare!" he exclaimed, "I didn't expect to meet you here."

"Nor did I think I should ever see you again," was the reply, as the girl extended her hand, which was grasped and shaken.

She was Ann Harbor, the daughter of the keeper of the Washington Hotel in Purvis, where Harvey had spent a night a short time before.

"Come in," said she hospitably; "Aunty will be as glad as me to see you."

Harvey stepped across the threshold into the living-room of the tidy dwelling. Seated at the opposite window was a small, neat, motherly-looking woman in spectacles engaged in sewing. She looked up with a winsome smile and greeted the visitor as his name was announced. She was Hephzibah Akers, sister of the landlord of the Washington Hotel, in Purvis, with whom her niece Ann was a favorite. Hat in one hand, the young aviator bowed and extended the other to the woman. She motioned him to a chair and expressed her pleasure in welcoming him to her humble home. After a few commonplaces, Harvey turned to Ann, who had also seated herself.

"You are quite a distance from Purvis?" he said inquiringly.

"Not so very far," she replied lightly; "Aunty doesn't come to see us often, so I run up to see her."

"I am not as young as she is," replied the elder, "and she is kind enough to come to see me, though not half as often as I should like to have her come."

"How long have you been here?" asked Harvey.

"I left home yesterday morning; bus'ness is dull with paw just now and he let me come up to Aunty's for a day or two. I shall have to go back to-morrow or next day. Now, how is it you are here when I thought you had gone to your home in New Jersey?"

The visitor had considered this question before it was asked. He decided that the best course was to be frank with the woman. So in a few words he told them that Professor Morgan had taken the colored lad with him, and since the aviator was known to be unbalanced in mind, Harvey was doing his utmost to get his friend away before it was too late. The story was so absorbing that Aunty ceased her sewing while she and her niece listened.

"I did go to my home," added Harvey, "but came back as soon as I could."

"Did you stay at our hotel last night?" asked Ann.

"No, your father likes the Professor better than he does me and I thought it best not to let any one know I was in the neighborhood."

"I guess you did right, for what you say is true. The night of the day you went away, the Professor stayed a good while at the hotel after supper and he and paw had a long talk. I was in and out of the room most of the time, so I heard nearly all they said. Paw told him you had gone off and we'd never see you agin; the Professor said it was lucky for you that you'd done so, for if you come round poking your nose into other people's bus'ness, you wouldn't live to try it a second time."

"Mercy!" exclaimed the shocked Aunty; "why did he say that?"

"'Cause he's crazy," was the prompt explanation of her niece.

"Ann is right the Professor has formed a plan which no one but a lunatic could think out; it is that of crossing the Atlantic Ocean with his aeroplane and of taking the colored boy with him. If they ever try it, it will be the last of both. I cannot rest idle if there is any way to prevent them."

"Of course not," assented Aunty; "it would be wicked if you didn't do your best to stop it. Can Ann and I help you?" she asked with such childlike simplicity that Harvey smiled.

"I see no way unless you have some information to give."

"I don't understand you."

"You have seen the Professor and his airship, I suppose?"

"Several times. I went to the spring on last Sunday morning for a pail of water, when the thing skimmed over my head so low that I ducked, though there wasn't any need."

"Which way was it traveling?"

"Straight north," she replied, indicating the direction by gesture.

"Did the man give any attention to you?"

"He didn't seem to see me, but was staring ahead, with his hands on the levers each side of him. He didn't look down, but the person with him did."

"Ah!" said the interested Harvey; "he had a companion then?"

"Yes; it must have been the young man you spoke of, for I remember he had a black face; he leaned over, waved his hand at me and shouted some words which I didn't catch. He was sitting beside the Professor."

"That was Bohunkus. When he and I sailed together, he never lost a chance of saluting every one who looked up at him. Now, Aunty, you tell me you saw an aerocar going northward; can you tell me how far it went?"

The woman shook her head.

"I watched him till my eyes ached. I can't see very well with my glasses and he soon passed out of sight."

"But what was his course?"

"Not exactly north, but a little to the east of north, toward Dix Peak and the Schroon River. He may have kept on to Nipple Top and Elizabethtown or even farther."

"What time of the day was this?"

"A little after breakfast. I was expecting Gideon and had waited for him, but he must have been too busy to come home."

"And may I know who Gideon is?"

"Why haven't you heard of Gid Akers?" asked the surprised niece; "he's one of the greatest guides in the Adirondacks. He is off now with a party, near Sanford Lake and Mount McMartin. He's been hired till the end of August, but manages to take a run down here once in awhile."

"You know I never was in the Adirondacks till the other day and really know nothing of them. You tell me, Aunty, that it was on Sunday morning that you saw the couple going northward in the airship. Did you see them return?"

"That was the funny part of it," replied the woman with a smile; "I was home alone all day, busy about the house, for I don't often get to church, when I went out again to the spring. I was dipping up water, when a queer shadow whisked over me and made me look up. There was the Professor, as you call him, going with the speed of the wind to the south."

"Alone?"

"Yes; he paid no more attention to me than before, though he must have seen me, but the seat beside him didn't hold any one."

This information was important, as confirming a part of Harvey Hamilton's theory: Professor Morgan had carried Bohunkus Johnson to some spot at an uncertain distance to the north, and left him there, with orders to stay until his master was ready to pick him up and start across the Atlantic.

"He went north again this morning," said the visitor, "and of course was alone."

"Where were you when you saw him?" asked the lady.

"On the other side of the ridge to the south, where I had hidden my aeroplane."

His listeners showed their astonishment.

"Have you got one of them things too?" asked Ann.

"I should have explained that I came all the way from home this second time in such a machine."

"Why didn't you come here in it?" asked Aunty; "I should dearly love to see one when it isn't whizzing like a bird through the air."

"You shall have a ride in mine, if it can possibly be arranged, and you too, Ann, for your kindness to me."

The big gray eyes sparkled.

"That will be bully—I mean splendaceous. Ain't you afeard something will happen to it, while you're gone?"

"I think not; it is well screened from sight, unless some one should happen to pass near. I was afraid to use it to come any farther lest the Professor should discover me. It is necessary that I should prevent that at all costs."

"Where did you stay last night?"

"In the woods with my aeroplane. You remember the weather was mild, and I was comfortable in my thick coat."

He did not think it worth while to tell them of his experience with the bear.

"Where did you have breakfast?"

"I didn't have any, and only a bite or two last night and, Ann, if you ever want to look upon a starving fellow, just take a good look at me."

CHAPTER X
AUNTY HEP TAKES A RIDE

THAT which followed these words was so amusing that Harvey Hamilton laughed outright. Aunty Hep dropped her sewing from her lap and sprang to her feet, with hands upraised in self-reproach.

"Mercy sakes alive! Poor boy! You are starving!"

In the same moment, Ann Harbor without speaking, darted into the small room at the rear which served as a kitchen. Evidently she believed in deeds more than in words.

"Not so bad as that, Aunty," protested the caller; "I am pretty hungry, but I can stand it a little longer. I shall be glad to eat a belated breakfast, but I beg you not to hurry."

"Not to hurry," she repeated reprovingly; "we can't hurry too much. You look pale and must feel faint. It won't take us long to get you something."

He protested again, but was not displeased by the promptness with which they met his need. Sooner than he expected, a bountiful meal was ready, and the coffee remaining in the pot was quickly reheated and a brimming cup poured out for him. They urged him to eat until he was compelled to stop. He dared not offer payment and thanked them over and over again. Their pleasure was as great as his own.

"I'm downright glad I didn't have my regular breakfast this morning," he said, when he shoved his chair back.

"Why?" asked the hostess.

"I should have lost the best meal I ever ate."

"La, now, you shouldn't say that."

"My mother taught me to speak the truth at all times; but Ann," he added, turning to the girl who was removing the dishes, "while you are helping like the good girl you are, I shall go outside to watch for the return of the Professor. It won't do to lose sight of him and he may come back at any time."

He walked across the floor and paused with his hand on the latch.

"If you don't mind, I'll go to my aeroplane, and when it is safe I shall bring it here for you and Aunty to look at."

With this understanding he set out on his return to the spot where he had left his machine. He was so grateful to the women that he was anxious to gratify them in every way possible, but he could not forget his simple-hearted friend who was in peril. More than an hour had passed since the Professor had winged his way northward and he was liable to return at any time or possibly he might wait for a long while. Harvey had already run great risk and could not be too careful.

He found that no one had been near the machine and it was as ready as ever for service. It would have been the height of imprudence for him to bring it forth so long as the return of the Professor was impending. He devoted a few minutes to oiling the moving parts and giving the structure a minute examination, and frequently he stepped into the open space and studied the sky through his field glass, searching for the object that had become familiar to him.

Remembering what Aunty Hep had said, he scrutinized the country a little to the east of north. It was mountainous, wooded, unsettled, and so far as he could judge contained very few or no cabins.

"It is the place where I should think he would hide Bunk, but his prison may be a score of miles beyond the farthest reach of my vision."

A mass of cumulous, fleecy clouds was drifting across the sky low down, while the firmament above was of a clear soft blue. Just below a stratum of snowy vapor, he saw what looked like a bird with outstretched wings sailing toward him. Its rapid increase in size and the power of the binoculars quickly disclosed the fact that it was a monoplane. Professor Morgan was returning to his workshop near the town of Purvis.

Instead of taking the same course as before, the inventor circled to the east, so that he was a fourth of a mile distant on his nearest approach to where Harvey Hamilton stood on the edge of the cleared space with leveled glass. He was still flying low, and in a few minutes sank from sight.

"I am sure that Detective Pendar would agree with me as to the meaning of what I have seen to-day. Professor Morgan carried food to Bunk, and at the same time gave his machine a test so far as he could. He has not yet accomplished all he has in mind, though he may be close to it, and has gone back to his workshop to continue his experiments. He will stay there for the rest of the day and make another trip to-morrow morning."

This was drawing it fine, but our young friend was so confident he was right that he acted upon the theory. It will be seen that he was steadily narrowing the circle of search. At daybreak he had established the fact that the place where Bunk was held a prisoner was north of the ridge which the pursuer crossed on his way to the home of Aunty Hephzibah Akers. He had learned later that it was somewhere in the wild region a little to the east of north, which loomed up on the farther limit of his vision. The next visit of the Professor to Bunk ought to locate the spot so nearly that Harvey could, so to speak, put his finger on it.

Aunt Hep had resumed her sewing by the window, and her niece having cleared off the table was chatting with her about the remarkable story told by their youthful caller, when both were startled by a roar and racket which caused them to listen with bated breath. Neither had ever heard anything like it, for it will be remembered that the monoplane to which they were accustomed sailed on its aerial voyages without ripple or noise. Ann sprang up and opened the door.

"O Aunty! here he is! come and look!"

As she called, she sprang off the little porch and ran out to where Harvey Hamilton had just finished volplaning to the earth only a few rods away from the front of the house. Her relative was at her heels, as much amazed as she. They stared at the strange looking thing, and upon the owner's invitation went forward and listened, absorbed, to his description of the functions of the different parts. Harvey patiently answered questions that belonged more to a child than to an adult.

"And now," he added, "I want you to take a ride with me."

They shrank back in dismay and shook their heads.

"I wouldn't do it for worlds!" gasped Aunty, and the awful thought caused her niece to whirl on her heel and plunge through the door into the house. A minute later she emerged again and hesitatingly approached the others.

"Nothing could make me expose you to the least danger," said Harvey soothingly; "I have ridden hundreds of miles in this and never been hurt; I know better how to handle it than ever before;

it is in the best condition and you need not have the slightest fear."

The result of his persistent persuasion was that the two consented to the venture which a half hour before they would not have faced for a fortune. He explained that they had only to sit still, after he had adjusted their seats so as to balance right, lightly grasp the rods at their side, and then fancy that the long-reaching arms were their own wings and they were two innocent birds coursing through the upper regions. Just as everything was ready, Ann was seized with sudden panic and would have leaped out, had not her relative caught her arm and sternly ordered her to keep her seat.

When, in response to the whirl of the propeller the machine began gliding down the slope, the girl screamed and her aunt had again to check her. Harvey sprang nimbly to his place and at the proper moment pointed the front rudder upward, and the aeroplane left the earth and soared into the heavens. The load being greater than usual he kept the propeller at its highest speed.

The young aviator proceeded on the principle of trying to kill two birds with one stone. He could give his friends the treat of their lives, but in doing so, he steered toward the point where he had first caught sight of the monoplane on its last return from the north. He had become so used to running the machine that he felt free to inspect the country while gliding over it. Before starting he had fixed the salient points in his mind, — the lofty peak to the westward, the endless stretch of wilderness, the villages and towns in the distance, the few scattered cabins, the ridge to the rear, the rushing, tumbling streams, and the lake a little way ahead and to his right. Scattered here and there were signs of life as shown by more than one canoe, gliding over the smooth waters, or paddled up the current or floating down it, with the fingers of vapor pointing skyward from the depths of the forests where parties of tourists or campers were gathered beneath. It was the glad summer time, and the visitors to the Adirondack region were numbered by the thousands. The open season was not much more than a month off when the hunters would shoot one another in the ardor of their pursuit of big game, with an occasional deer thrown in as a counterpoise to their mistakes.

With some misgiving as to how his passengers would stand what was certainly an ordeal, Harvey looked around at them. Each was tightly grasping the support at her side, and they sat as rigid as statues, their faces pale, but the glow of their eyes showing how entranced they were with the flight and how keen was their enjoyment of it. When Ann's eyes met those of her friend, she shook her head and tried to smile, but did not make much of a success of it. Exalted as were her emotions when she gazed down at the wonderfully picturesque landscape sweeping past, she longed to feel it once more under her feet.

Harvey did not overdo matters. He flew ten or twelve miles, which he was sure took him to the point in his mind. He peered below but saw only trees, masses of rocks and a small waterfall, but no sign of life.

"Now if Bunk is down there, as I believe he is, he ought to notice this biplane. Likely he is looking at me this very minute."

Prompted by the fancy Harvey took off his cap and swung it round his head, searching the earth below in the hope of catching a response.

"He is so ready to do that sort of thing he ought to reply. As I am carrying two passengers he might not recognize me, but that need not prevent his answering my salutation."

The solitude remained as unbroken, however, as at "creation's morn," and afraid to go any farther, Harvey made a wide curve to the right and began his return.

Although he had not caught a sign of Bohunkus Johnson, he saw others. Two men standing on the bank of the uppermost tributary of the Schroon discharged their guns. They could have done no harm had they been pointed at the aeroplane, for the distance was too great, but the weapons were aimed at nothing and the action was meant as a salute to the navigator of the air. He saw the gray puffs and waved his cap as the only thing he could do by way of acknowledgment. A man paddling up stream in a canoe held the blade motionless and circled his hat, while his two feminine companions waved their handkerchiefs and doubtless said something appropriate to the occasion.

The large white tent to which allusion has been made and which stood on the shore of the small lake, was hardly a mile from the home of Aunt Hephzibah Akers. The young aviator sailed almost directly over it, leaning well to one side and peering downward, but the camp appeared to be deserted. He decided that the campers were off on a tramp or fishing excursion.

From this point to the little patch of ground in front of the home of Gideon Akers, the guide, was so slight a distance that in a minute or so, Harvey spiraled down as gracefully as an alighting bird, on the spot where he had halted before. The women sighed with relief and enjoyment as he helped them to the ground. They were grateful and urged him to spend the remainder of the day at the house.

Harvey would have done so but for the feeling that it would be neglecting the interests of Bunk. Aunt Hep herself had commended his vigorous earnestness, but the question which he asked himself was whether to lay aside his aeroplane at this point or to return to where he had wheeled about when he came back. If he did the latter he would advance that much nearer Bohunkus, but his scrutiny of the ground had not disclosed a suitable spot for landing. He feared he would be caught at a disadvantage and find his machine useless when he needed it the most. He decided upon a compromise. He would leave the aeroplane at the home of Aunt Hep, and since more than half the day remained, press on afoot.

Accordingly he pushed the machine to the rear of the dwelling, where a shed gave shelter to the single cow whenever she was in want of it, and managed to screen the biplane from sight provided no one's suspicion was drawn to the spot. Then he bade his friends good-bye for the time and started off on a tramp that was destined to bring him an experience of which he little dreamed.

CHAPTER XI
THE CAMPERS

AS midday approached, the weather grew warmer. Harvey Hamilton left his traveling bag at the home of Aunt Hephzibah Akers, since he did not intend to journey far, and it would be easy to go back when necessary. Most of the distance between him and the tent on the edge of the lake was a gradual slope downward, through the usual underbrush and around occasional rocks and boulders, but the traveling, on the whole, was not difficult, and he made fair progress. He doffed his outer coat and slung it over an arm as a sort of balance to the field glass suspended by a cord from the opposite shoulder.

He remembered that when he peeped down from his aeroplane he saw no signs of any one near the tent, but if the owners had gone on a tramp as he supposed, some of them had returned during the brief interval. While drawing near along the beach he saw a man a little to one side of the primitive dwelling, where he had started a fire and was evidently preparing the noonday meal. His companion lifted the flap, stooped, and was in the act of passing from sight when Harvey caught his first good view of the tent from the ground. A little later the other person came out. This brought him face to face with Harvey when about a hundred paces separated them. The back of his companion was toward the caller of whose coming as yet he was not aware.

Harvey had noticed that they were attired in modern camping costume, with leggings, gray flannel shirts, and caps instead of hats. A gaudy handkerchief was knotted loosely about the neck and dangled over the shirt front, across which the big red letters "C A & W E S" could be traced, as far as the young men themselves were distinguishable.

The one who confronted Harvey looked at him for an instant, and then touched the forefinger of his hand to his cap in military salute. The visitor returned it and pushed on. The second camper heard his footfall and wheeled around.

"How do you do, sir?" he called. "We're glad to see you."

They both offered their hands as Harvey went forward. He was won by their hospitality and cheeriness of manner. He explained:

"I am Harvey Hamilton, from Mootsport, New Jersey, and I have come to the Adirondacks on a strange errand in which perhaps you can help me."

"It will give us pleasure to do so," replied the one with the briarwood. As he made this answer Harvey distinctly saw him wink at his companion, who returned the trivial and yet often significant signal. The young aviator was mystified, for he suspected instinctively that something was back of it.

"We are sophomores at Yale, and are up here on a little outing. My name is Val Hunter, and I am from Vicksburg, Mississippi. This ugly looking tramp with me is Fred Wadsworth, from the wilds of western New York. We have a third member who sneaked off with our boat this morning and there's no saying when we shall see him again."

"I have a brother who is a sophomore at Yale," said Harvey; "and he is or was a short time ago somewhere in the Adirondacks. You must know him."

"What is his front name?"

"Dick."

The two looked at each other and Hunter said: "I recall him and there isn't a more popular fellow in college. He can box, row, play baseball and football, and leads his class in his studies."

Harvey's heart warmed to the Southerner.

"I can't tell you how glad I am to hear you say that; something of the same nature has come to us at home and father and mother are proud enough, but Dick never tells us anything about himself."

"We tried to get him to go with us on this trip, but a party of seniors dragged him off. He was very sorry to part with us and wouldn't have done so but for his promise made earlier. We are honored in having his brother with us and beg he will make more than a short call."

Harvey was sure he had never met two finer gentlemen. Val Hunter was a true specimen of the aristocratic Southerner, with his black hair and eyes, olive complexion, now darkened by tan, and his lithe, sinewy limbs. His words were marked by the slight drawl now and then and the suppressed "r" which often mark the speech of those born and reared south of Mason and Dixon's Line. His companion, Wadsworth, from New York, was of stumpy build, with a round ruddy face, also well tanned, light gray eyes and inveterate good-nature, but by no means as comely in looks as Hunter. It was evident that they were attached to each other, probably on the principle of like and unlike being drawn together.

In front of the tent and a little to one side, a short decayed log had been rolled. This was useful as well as convenient. When the young men wished to smoke they could use it, if they preferred to sit rather than loll on the bare ground. Besides, if they needed a table for their plates when eating, here it was, though an up-ended box served them oftener.

"I was about to prepare dinner," said Hunter, "It being my day for such menial duty, but it is early and we can sit for awhile. Have one?"

He handed a package of cigarettes to Harvey, who thanked him and shook his head.

"Father and Dick do the smoking for our family."

"You'll be along in time," replied the other; "cigarettes aren't good for some folks and I'm one of 'em, which explains why I smoke 'em. You know that's the basic principle of human nature; the way to make a person do a thing is first to convince him he shouldn't do it. It shines out in those beautiful lines of Shakespeare or Milton, I forget which:

'I ne'er would have been in this condition

But for mother's prohibition.'"

"That's clever in its way, because of the profound truth involved," remarked the New Yorker, "but for fine, delicate fancy it does not equal that quatrain:

'This road is not passable,

It is hardly jackassable,

And you who do travel it

Should turn to and gravel it.'"

Harvey laughed at the solemn manner in which this nonsense was delivered. Nodding toward Wadsworth he asked:

"What do those letters mean?"

The other smiled.

"That reminds me of a day when I saw a scorer in the grandstand at the ball grounds ruling off and writing captions on his card. With much twisting of his mouth he scrawled the word 'Ares.' I asked him what it meant. With a look of pitying scorn he answered: 'Why them's errors.' It is with something of the same emotion that I reply to your question: Those letters signify 'Champions of the Adirondacks and the Whole Empire State.'"

"If your modesty strikes in," said Harvey, catching the spirit of the moment, "it will be fatal."

"That's what we're afraid of, but wait till you meet the Duke."

"And who is the Duke?"

"I beg pardon for not explaining before. His full title is Duke de Sassy. He really is a poor Cracker from Florida, who has such a hard time getting through the University that several of us are paying his expenses on the dead quiet."

"Has he much ability?"

It was the Southerner who took it upon himself to reply:

"Below the average, which makes it all the harder for him. Wadsworth and I, out of pity, invited him to go with us on this outing. Florida is a mighty poor place in the summer season."

"Or any other season," amended Wadsworth.

"We were glad to do so, but it galls us to fail to see the first spark of gratitude or appreciation on his part. Not once has he said so much as 'Thank you' for all the favors done him."

"It is hardly fair to refer to his prodigious appetite and I shall not do so further than to say that it has doubled our expenses."

"I hope you don't begrudge him his food," said Hunter reprovingly to his friend, whose slur struck him as in poor taste.

"Of course not; it's our food that I dislike to see appropriated by him."

"I suppose the treat is so rare a one for him," suggested Harvey, "that he cannot help making the most of it."

"There may be something in that," replied Wadsworth, "but the fellow is absent and it doesn't seem fair to abuse him when he can't reply, though what we have just said has been said to his face."

"How does he take it?"

"Grins and eats more than ever. Which reminds me that the Adirondacks seem to have become a favorite tramping ground for airships. Two of them are hovering over and about us."

"Yes," remarked Hunter, "and we saw a rarity to-day. We were fishing when a biplane sailed overhead with two women as passengers."

"Did you recognize the aviator?" asked Harvey.

"How should we?"

"It was myself."

"No!" exclaimed the Southerner, and he and his companion stared in astonishment at their caller; "you don't mean it?"

"It was certainly myself and the two ladies belong to that house up yonder at the head of the lake. I came to this section from New Jersey, covering the whole distance in my aeroplane, and I expect to return the same way, but with only one passenger. My machine awaits me at the house of Guide Ackers."

Thereupon Harvey told his story, which it need not be said was listened to with deep interest by his new friends.

"I never heard of anything stranger," commented Hunter; "that crazy inventor whom you call Professor Morgan has been in these parts for nearly a week. We must help you to get the colored boy away from him."

"I shall be glad if you can, for from what I have told you he is in imminent peril. You understand that the first necessity is to locate the prison where he holds the poor fellow."

"By George!" exclaimed Wadsworth, slapping his knee; "don't you remember, Val, that the first time we saw the machine sailing overhead there were two persons in it?"

"You are right; we were sitting on this very log with the Duke, all three smoking and talking of nothing in particular, when the Duke caught sight of the thing well over toward the other side of the lake. He dived into the tent, brought out his binoculars and we all took a squint at it. It was going very fast and the man on the driving seat sat up very straight with his hands on the wheel and his feet down in front."

"That was the Professor," said Harvey.

"We couldn't make out whether the one sitting beside him was colored or not. He must have fancied we were watching him, for he waved his cap at us and we returned the salute."

"That was Bunk: he always does that. Now, how long did you watch the monoplane?"

"As long as it was in sight. It returned later in the day and went back over the same course, but it carried only one person."

"That confirms the theory I formed some time ago. Professor Morgan was afraid to have Bunk with him at his workshop, because he might change his mind and run away, or could be found more readily by his friends. So he took him to some place out yonder, where he intends he shall stay until he is ready to start on the maddest trip an aviator ever dreamed of. Now can you tell me how far the Professor went with his machine?"

"I had the glass and was standing right here watching him," replied Wadsworth. "Up among those rocks and trees which you see a little to the left and six or eight miles away, the machine seemed to come to a stop and to hang motionless in the air, but that could not be."

"That is exactly what you saw; the Professor has invented what he calls an 'uplifter,' which is nothing more than a horizontal propeller under the engine, by which he can hold himself stationary when he wishes."

"I was so puzzled by the sight that I handed the glass to the Duke, who laughed at what he called my fancy. But when he had looked it was his turn to be surprised, for he couldn't see any aeroplane at all. It had vanished as completely as if it had dived into a hole in the ground. He passed the glass back to me, but I was no more successful than he. Then Val tried it with the same result."

"You knew what that meant?" said Harvey inquiringly. "There was no mystery about it."

"I presume the aviator made a landing among the trees."

"His uplifter enables him to descend where he chooses, for he can come as straight down as a stone falling from the sky. A space a few yards wide will answer and there must be plenty of such spots even in so wild a region as that beyond us."

"That must be the explanation," said Hunter, "and of course he can make the same kind of start, though we have never seen him do it. We couldn't afford to wait here until he came back, but have noticed him several times since."

"Hello! that must be the Duke!" said Wadsworth as the three heard the sound of whistling from the wood on the other side of the tent.

"Brace yourself to meet this undesirable citizen," added Hunter, lowering his voice; "try to bear with him, for he needs your charity. He's a 'bad egg.'"

The next moment the third member of the little party, still whistling a popular air, came into view from behind the tent and Wadsworth, who had risen, said impressively:

"Mr. Hamilton, permit me to introduce you to the Duke de Sassy, a general nuisance and—"

CHAPTER XII
BROTHER DICK

THE tall, handsome young man who came into view and who had been referred to as "Duke de Sassy" stopped short, his music nipped in two, and for an instant stood speechless. It was the same with Harvey Hamilton, who stared as if unable to believe his eyes. Val Hunter and Fred Wadsworth doubled over with laughter, and dropped on the log behind them.

The latest arrival was the first to regain his self-command. It was a gasp rather than an exclamation:

"Well, I'll be hanged!"

"Dick, as sure as I'm alive!" responded Harvey, rushing forward and grasping the hand of his elder brother, who dropped the string of fish he was carrying, and flinging an arm over the shoulders of the younger, pressed him to his breast. There could be no mistaking the affection of the two for each other, and both Hunter and Wadsworth felt ashamed of the harmless trick played their caller. They abruptly stopped their merriment and the Southerner swallowed a lump in his throat. He had once been blessed with a younger brother, but kissed him their long, last farewell two years before. Wadsworth had never passed through the sorrowful experience, but he saw the emotion of his friend and respected it.

Dick and Harvey shook hands several times, laughed, slapped each other on the back, and asked and answered numerous questions before they awoke to the fact that others were near. Harvey had to tell about home and all the news concerning the folks. Neither they nor Harvey had thought of the brothers meeting, though it would seem that the fact that Harvey's destination was the Adirondacks, where Dick was known to be, ought to have suggested the possibility of such a thing.

Grouped at the front of the tent the four youths had a merry chat, for all were in high spirits.

"The minute I looked at Harvey," said Hunter, "I noticed his resemblance to Dick, but did not suspect the relationship until he gave his name. Then Fred and I knew before he furnished any more particulars that you were brothers. Since the Duke was absent, we felt it our duty to acquaint Harvey with a few facts about his big brother, though the task was anything but pleasant."

"It seemed to give both of you a mighty lot of pleasure," said Harvey, who was so glad to see Dick that he reached over and shook hands with him again.

"Possibly you are correct, though we tried to keep down all signs of it, which reminds me that the dinner hour is approaching and even now is at hand."

It being the turn of Hunter to serve in the culinary department, he sprang to his feet, walked over to where Dick Hamilton had dropped his string of mountain bass and carried them to the edge of the lake, where he began dressing and preparing them for the fire, which was burning briskly in the rough stone stove whose pattern, you will recall, was described in the "Catamount Series."

All three of the young men were the sons of well-to-do parents and they went into the Adirondacks fully equipped for their outing of a month or more. The guide, Gideon Akers, had helped them in transporting their tent luggage and provisions, consisting of sugar, coffee, tea, prepared flour, condiments, ham, condensed milk, etc., and the necessary cooking utensils. After camp was made, the professional guide left, to fill an engagement with a larger party which penetrated much farther into the wilderness. That all were provided with firearms followed as a matter of course. Each carried a Colt's six-shooter, in addition to which Dick Hamilton had a small Winchester rifle. He needed no reminder that the game protectors in the Adirondacks are keen in their work, and it would have been very imprudent for him to shoot any big game during the close season. He had no intention of doing so, but he might need the larger weapon in some emergency.

When he wrote home to his father that he was on the trail of a gigantic buck, he told a partial truth. He had met such an animal twice, and knew its favorite haunt was in that region. The temptation to run the risk of bagging him was strong, and if all the circumstances were favorable, he was not sure he would not take a shot at him, though how to get the antlers home was a grave problem likely to involve him in difficulty, with the loss of the trophy and a tremendous fine to pay. However, that was a question which may be dismissed for the present.

As the three were seated on the log, Harvey told again the story of Professor Morgan, the cranky inventor, and the missing Bohunkus Johnson. The negro lad was strongly liked by Dick as well as his brother, and the sympathies of the elder were roused. He insisted that no thought or attention should be given to anything else until the colored youth was rescued from what beyond question was a situation of gravest danger.

"And I can lead you almost to the spot," added Dick. "As you know, I went off early this morning in the canoe which I drew up in the little inlet behind the tent where you didn't see me. I paddled to the farther end of the lake to fish in a splendid spot and was there when that monoplane sailed by and dropped down among the rocks and trees not more than half a mile away."

"Did you notice where it landed?" asked Harvey.

"Not precisely, for my position was so low that it dropped out of sight before coming down, but I can hit it pretty closely. What is your plan, Harv?"

"Let us all start for the section as soon as we have finished dinner, and then scatter and begin our search. We can't miss it."

A difficulty presented itself. The canoe was not buoyant enough to carry the four, though possibly it might bear three. It was six miles at least to the end of the lake and the tramp was a hard one because of the roughness of the country, while the water offered the easiest kind of a passage. Dick struck the solution. Addressing Val Hunter and Fred Wadsworth he said:

"There is not the slightest need of you going with us. Harv and I will paddle to the northern end. We shall then be quite near where there is every reason to believe Bunk is a prisoner. When it isn't best to paddle any farther we shall pull the canoe up into the bushes and hide it. Then Harv and I will separate. We know how to signal to Bunk, who will recognize the call and answer it. If the Professor doesn't come back and interfere it will be as easy as rolling off a log."

"That shuts us out altogether," said Hunter, "which we don't like."

"Not by a large majority," added Wadsworth.

"I shall leave the glass with you, and when the monoplane comes in sight you can study every movement and quite likely pick up useful information."

The proposal did not give the two much comfort, but it was really the right thing to do. Provided the brothers landed near Bunk, it ought to be as easy for two to locate him as it would be for a score of searchers. He had been an old friend of Dick and Harvey from earliest childhood, and they knew all his peculiarities. Held, as he no doubt was, under the spell of the Professor's domineering brain, he might shrink from trusting himself in the care of strangers. It was not unlikely, as the brothers viewed it, that he would keep out of sight of Hunter and Wadsworth, having no knowledge of why they sought him, or whether they meant well, but it would be the other way when he recognized his old friends.

This being explained to Val and Fred they accepted it and the plan was agreed upon before the midday meal was concluded. Dick led the way to the tiny inlet at the rear of the tent, where the pretty little canoe had been drawn up the bank. He carried his rifle and a full supply of cartridges with him and had also his revolver, as did Harvey.

"I don't suppose you have had occasion to use it yet?" said the elder inquiringly, while they paused for a minute or two to admire the graceful craft in front of them.

Harvey shrunk from telling the story of his meeting with the bear.

"I haven't fired it off since leaving home," he said.

"It isn't likely you will have to do so," remarked the elder, with no suspicion of the whole truth, "but it is well to be prepared. Step in."

The canoe had been shoved into the water and Harvey carefully seated himself in the bow, though there was no difference in the fashion of the ends, except in the arrangement of the seats. Dick followed, first handing his gun to Harvey, who, having left his outer coat in camp, had nothing more to look after. The elder had had more experience in handling the ashen paddle, which he manipulated in Indian fashion, dipping the broad blade in the water on one side and drawing it back with a powerful sweep and outward twist of the wrists at the end of the stroke, which kept the canoe on an even course. Harvey, seated in the bow with his back to Dick, handled his paddle in a similar fashion on the other side of the craft.

The task of propelling the boat was so light and everything around so quiet that the two said much to each other. They had a great deal in common and talked of many things, of no interest to any one else.

"You did mighty well, Harv," said Dick, softly swinging the paddle from which the water silently dripped, "in tracking the Professor to the Adirondacks. We get the papers now and then in camp and read of the kidnapping case of the Philadelphia merchant's child, but with never a thought that you were mixed up in it. After plucking this dark-hued brand from the burning, why not make it your profession? You can skyhoot around the country in your airboat and hunt out such jobs."

"I'll think it over, Dick, but I don't see much profit in it. Detective Pendar offered to divide the reward with me, but I couldn't think of that."

"Of course not; Bunk hasn't much wealth and I don't believe Mr. Hartley will give more than twenty-five cents to get him back again."

"That would hardly pay for the gasoline and oil, to say nothing of my own keep."

"But think of the fun you would have. When this business is finished I should like to try that aeroplane."

"I shall be glad to give you and your friends all the air excursions you would like."

"To get down to serious business, Harv, I see only one thing that stands in the way of our success."

"What is that?"

"I am sure you are right in believing the Professor spends all his spare time in his workshop, and visits Bunk only to carry him food and to see that he stays where he put him. But he may complete his plans sooner than we are figuring upon and make his start for Africa before we can get our hands on Bunk."

"It may be so, but I haven't much fear of it. He will have to take enough food to last them two or three days and you know something of Bunk's appetite."

It will be borne in mind that the canoe was moving toward the northern end of the lake, in which direction the two occupants faced. Before them was the section in which they hoped to find their missing friend. Their backs were turned upon the workshop of Professor Morgan in the neighborhood of the little town of Purvis. When last seen he was traveling in that direction, and the brothers ought not to have forgotten to watch the sky to the south. None the less they did so and the oversight proved unfortunate.

Harvey said something which Dick did not fully catch. Without ceasing to swing his paddle, he turned his head, glanced over his shoulder and asked for a repetition of the words. Before the younger could comply, Dick said in an excited undertone:

"Cover your face with your handkerchief, Harv!"

The younger was quickwitted enough to obey without stopping an instant to learn the reason for the strange command. He snatched out the piece of silk and held it to his nose in a natural manner and awaited the explanation which he knew would come in a second or two.

At the moment of looking back, Dick Hamilton saw the monoplane coming with the speed of a hurricane barely fifty feet aloft and directly over them. Professor Morgan had noticed the two young men in the canoe and a tinge of suspicion caused him to sail thus low that he might gain a look at the faces of the occupants. Since the elder brother was a stranger to him, it was better that his countenance should be clearly seen, but one glimpse of the face of Harvey would reveal everything. If he bowed his head to hide his features the act would be significant, but calling into play his handkerchief had nothing singular about it. To give naturalness to the action, Harvey emitted a blast from his nasal organ which suggested the honk of an automobile horn. In the uninterrupted stillness the aviator probably heard it.

Dick gazed aloft and watched the swoop of the machine with the strange man controlling the levers, who leaned forward and over, and scrutinized the couple so keenly that Dick caught the gleam of the piercing black eyes, and circled his dripping paddle about his shoulders by way of salutation; but the Professor made no acknowledgment. He continued to peer sharply downward until he had shot well past, when he curved upward and continued his swift course over the sheet of water and the wooded country beyond. It could not be seen that he glanced again behind him but skimmed away with undiminished swiftness.

CHAPTER XIII
DISCOVERY IMPENDS

HARVEY asked in a muffled voice: "May I take away my handkerchief?"

"It can do no harm, but I don't know that your precaution did any good."

"I kept my eyes open and peeped over the top; the way the Professor studied us proved he had misgivings, but he did not see my features."

"It looks as if he is not satisfied."

The elder referred to the fact that the aviator, instead of veering to the left and coming to a stop as he had done earlier in the day, continued his straightaway course. Harvey unshipped his field glass and leveled it at the object which rapidly grew smaller and finally flickered from sight.

"He is doing that to mislead us," said Harvey.

"Is there any way by which we can make him believe he has succeeded?"

"How would it do to stop paddling and begin fishing if he comes into sight again?"

"I am proud of a brother bright enough to think of that; it is a good plan, for if he is not satisfied he will come back for another view and he mustn't catch us napping."

Accordingly the paddle was swung again, and the younger brother gave his attention to watching the sky in every direction, for it was possible that with so swift a machine as was at his command the Professor might make a wide circuit and swoop down upon them again from the rear.

"If he does," said Harvey, "it will show that he doesn't like the look of things, and if I resort to my handkerchief again he will know why I do so."

"Which will be as bad as if you didn't do it. If we can reach the end of the lake before he returns we'll begin our hunt without more delay, but—"

"By George! Yonder he comes!"

"Quick! Get out your fishing line; I always carry mine."

Dick dropped the paddle in the bottom of the canoe and in a twinkling had flung the sinker into the crystalline water. It took Harvey a little longer, but he did it, with a number of seconds to spare. They could well affect not to be aware of the aerocar, though it was sailing low down, since it moved silently, and true fishermen are always absorbed in the work, or rather pleasure, of trying to woo a bite from the finny inhabitants below the surface. Neither seemed to look up, but none the less they kept a stealthy watch for the monoplane in which they were interested.

Professor Morgan gave a thrilling exhibition of his machine's capability and his skill in handling it. He made a sweeping curve which took him past the fishermen, swooping gracefully to the right and to the left at a height of less than a hundred feet. When he was nearest them he shouted:

"Hello, there! What are you doing?"

Harvey Hamilton just then was excitedly pulling at his line as if he had a bite and was more anxious to land his catch than to do anything else. Dick suspended his occupation and looked up.

"Can't you see we are fishing?" was his fitting reply in the form of a question.

"You are watching me," insisted the aviator, as he made another circle and came nearer.

"What do we care about you? You are scaring away the fish; I wish you would clear out and leave us alone."

"Who is that with you?"

"Bill Jones, from Squedunk; he hasn't much sense and if you don't look out he'll take a shot at you with his revolver, and if he doesn't I will!"

And Dick dropped his fishing line over the edge of the canoe, picked up his rifle and pointed it at the loony inventor.

"Get!" he commanded, "before I fire!"

The demonstration was unexpected, and scared Professor Morgan. Had it not been done at the psychological moment, it is likely he would have approached still closer and forced Harvey to disclose himself. The youth was in a tremor, but it was hard for him to restrain his merriment over the rank bluffing of his brother. The Professor yanked his levers and with his feet abruptly turned the rudder so that his machine shot off at a tangent at an amazing rate of speed. Instead of turning back over his course, he made for the wooded, rocky, mountainous country which had been his destination when he believed he was not under the eye of any one. As soon as he was beyond distinct vision, Harvey dropped his fishing line and brought his field glass into use.

"Keep an eye on him as long as he's in sight," warned Dick, who also laid his line aside and turned to watch the aviator. The latter held to a direct course for half a mile or more, by which time he was above the section where the brothers believed Bohunkus Johnson was kept in confinement.

"He seems to have stopped," said Dick.

"He has; he is descending."

Holding his machine in poise for a minute or two, Harvey saw it dropping down like a weight suspended at the end of a rope. It disappeared behind a mass of rocks and amid a group of large trees covered with exuberant foliage.

"It looks as if that is the spot for which we are hunting," said Harvey lowering the glass.

"All the same it isn't; it's a trick meant to make us believe it is. Professor Morgan may be crazy regarding aeroplanes, but he isn't in a good many other things. It has become a game of hide and seek between us."

Conceding this to be the truth, our young friends had to decide upon their next step.

"If we land and go to the place, he will know we are more interested in him than he thinks we ought to be. He is watching us from where he landed."

"And if we go there we shall not find Bunk. I do not think he is anywhere near. Meanwhile, the best thing we can do is to keep on fishing. Doubtless he has a glass and is scrutinizing us like a cat watching a mouse. Let's drop our lines into the water."

They did so and a minute later Harvey felt a tug at his hook. Drawing in his line, he landed a plump bass that must have weighed nearly two pounds.

"If the Professor has noticed that," remarked the younger, "it will help him to believe we are no more than we pretend to be; but, Dick, I don't understand why he doesn't shut us off from interfering with him."

"How would he do it?"

"Pick up Bunk and carry him away."

"Where to?"

"He could keep him in his workshop for the little while that must pass before he starts on his grand flight."

"The Professor is shrewd enough to know the risk he will run. He took him away from that place because he was afraid Bunk would give him the slip. It would require too much of the Professor's time to watch Bunk and hold him under his thumb. Besides, what is to prevent our hurrying to Dawson or some other nearby town and securing a writ of habeas corpus from a judge which would require the Professor to produce the body of Bunk in court and explain why he is held in durance, —I believe that's the way they put it. Such a proceeding would not only be highly unpleasant to the Professor but would be followed by more unpleasant ones, —such as a lunacy commission to look into his own affairs. The aerial trip across the Atlantic would be knocked higher than Gilderoy's kite."

"If he is afraid to keep Bunk in his workshop, he can take him to any one of a score of places where he would be as well hidden as now."

"That is what I'm afraid of. It seems to me we played our parts so well that very little suspicion is left in the Professor's mind. Were it otherwise he would shift Bunk's temporary home, though it isn't likely he can hit at once upon one that is as satisfactory."

"Then for the present we must continue to be fishermen."

"So it strikes me, and if he is observing us closely he will admit that we are giving a very good imitation of fishermen," added Dick as he drew in a bass almost as large as his brother's. "You are facing the spot where you last saw him; give that as much attention as you do your line."

Thus the situation remained for more than half an hour, during which two more fish were landed. It irked the brothers thus to sit idle, with the soft summer afternoon slipping past and the minutes going by unimproved. When they left camp it was with high hopes of bringing Bunk back before nightfall, but the prospect looked doubtful.

Suddenly Harvey saw a peculiar flickering agitation behind the rocks where the monoplane had disappeared.

"Something's up!" he whispered, letting his line fall and bringing his glass again into play. "The Professor is bestirring himself."

First the widespread wings of the monoplane rose slowly into sight; the powerful engine, slender body and rudders at the rear following. The uplifter was doing duty and the Dragon of the Skies climbed the aerial stairway smoothly and silently.

"See whether he has Bunk with him," cautioned Dick, looking keenly in the same direction; "that's the important point."

"By George! he has!" exclaimed Harvey; "I see him plainly!"

"Let me have a look!"

Harvey passed the instrument to his brother, who hastily leveled it at the machine. "You can't miss him," added the younger; "he is sitting in his old place on the seat beside the Professor, who is so tall that his head rises far over Bunk's."

Dick was silent for a brief while. Suddenly he lowered the glass with a laughing exclamation.

"Ah, but the Professor is sly. I see the form behind him as you have described, but it isn't Bohunkus Johnson!"

"What do you mean?" asked the amazed Harvey.

"Study it out for yourself," replied the other, handing over the instrument.

A few seconds' scrutiny was enough. That which Harvey had taken for their colored friend was a cunningly arranged dummy which might well deceive a spectator. Professor Morgan had adjusted a coat and other garments so as to resemble the form of the negro and make the mistake almost certain. But for the keener shrewdness of his brother, Harvey would have been deceived.

"I see what you mean, Dick; I hadn't the first suspicion of such a trick."

"We are not dealing with a fool when we butt against the Professor."

"He keeps going toward Purvis," said Dick, who had once more resorted to his field glass; "he seems to be certain he has misled us."

"Why shouldn't he be? His last view showed him we were fishing as hard as ever and he must believe we shall not figure any more in his affairs."

"Well, Dick, we must be up and doing if we expect to help Bunk."

"True; we are through fishing for the present."

They flung the lines down in the boat, Dick took up the paddle.

"If we have to camp out to-night, we shall have our supper with us. There's some consolation in that. I don't believe the Professor will show up again before to-morrow morning. He may have his invention completed by that time, but everything must remain guesswork for awhile."

Under the propulsion of the paddle the light craft skimmed swiftly over the placid lake. Dick put forth all his skill and the canoe touched the shingle a few minutes later and both stepped ashore and drew the boat up the shore.

"It strikes me, Harv, that it will be better for us to separate. We don't know whether to hunt for Bunk at the place where the Professor halted awhile ago, or to look for him farther over to the right where I have seen his machine several times."

"I should say that the spot you saw is most likely the right one."

"So it seems to me, but the afternoon is so far gone that we shall need every minute and we mustn't go too far astray. It's a safe guess that one of us will establish communication with Bunk pretty soon."

Further discussion made it seem that the section selected by Dick was about a fourth of a mile to the east of the other. Thus it would not become necessary for them to lose mutual touch. Like all boys accustomed to hunt and wander together in the woods, they had a system of signaling by means of whistling. Bunk was also familiar with the code. The three had made their wishes known when a mile apart.

"If you find him," said Dick, "whistle three times and I'll do the same if I succeed."

"Suppose both fail?"

"When it becomes too dark to hunt longer, I'll call to you; you will answer in our usual way and each will tramp toward the other. Then we'll make camp and start in again at daybreak."

It was agreed that in case either met the Professor or ran into danger and needed help, he would summon it by five or six short sharp blasts from his lips.

"You have your rifle and I only my revolver, so I shall be more likely to need you," said Harvey as the brothers parted company.

120

CHAPTER XIV
A NATURAL PRISON

OUR young friend Harvey Hamilton often recalled the words of Detective Simmons Pendar. One remark impressed him when his course diverged from that of his brother, and they passed from the sight of each other. Whenever a crime or bit of wrongdoing comes to light, the officers whose duty it is to bring the guilty ones to justice proceed to formulate their theories. Their guesswork is often ingenious to the degree of brilliancy, and an error seems impossible. The skeins when unraveled must make clear everything as was promised at the beginning.

And yet it not infrequently comes about that the whole theory turns out to be a rope of sand. It crumbles and truth assumes a wholly new guise. The brothers had done a good deal of guessing and might be far astray. It seemed to them that the missing Bohunkus Johnson would be found either near the spot where Professor Morgan had made his last descent and rise, or at the other place not far off where Dick Hamilton had seen the monoplane more than once. And still it was possible that the colored youth was not within miles of either locality.

Since, however, the two had no other basis upon which to act, they promptly set out to test the truth of their guesses. Although they were not far from settlements, towns, villages and camps of visitors in the wilderness, both straightway plunged into the wildest section of the southern Adirondacks. Harvey found the steeply ascending surface so precipitous that it was often hard work to force his way forward. Rarely could he do so in a straight line, and he was obliged to make many long, laborious detours, but he had a fine perception of direction, and a glance at the lake and country behind him prevented any confusion of the points of the compass. So arduous was his work that a full hour passed before he believed he was near the spot where the monoplane last halted. He was in doubt for some time, but finally identified the vast pile of rocks, with the exuberant growth of underbrush and trees only a little way beyond.

"This is the place," he decided, after some time spent in inspection; "over yonder is where the machine was hidden from sight for awhile. I am sure I am not mistaken, though it remains to be seen whether the discovery will do any good."

Nothing striking was observed when he looked around. Working his way to the right of the pile of stones, his eye rested upon an open space only a few rods in area, just beyond and between the rocks and the trunks of the trees. The decayed leaves on the bottom proved that not long before vegetation had taken root in the spot, but some cause which he did not understand had obliterated all traces of it.

An examination of the ground showed a disturbance of the leaves as if made by the feet of a person, and closer scrutiny disclosed where the small rubber-tired wheels of the monoplane had pressed. Unquestionably the young aviator had come upon the place for which he was searching.

But where was Bohunkus Johnson? Harvey saw nothing to suggest a cavern or the rudest kind of shelter. He groped here and there, but the search was unavailing. It might be, however, that the machine had descended at this point because no other near at hand would serve.

Harvey had hesitated through a strange dread of disappointment to appeal to the help that was his from the first.

He now inserted his thumb and forefinger between his lips and sent out two resounding blasts which were twice repeated, the last closing with a queer tremolo that may be said to have been the highest attainment of the art of signaling. Only he, his brother and Bunk had mastered this crowning achievement.

"If that reaches Bunk's ears he will know from whom it comes," reflected Harvey in the attitude of intense listening.

From some point a long way off sounded the faint report of a gun; he heard the shout of a person answered by that of another; the soft breeze rustled the foliage overhead, but there was nothing more. Then he again repeated the calls, but in vain; not the slightest suggestion of a reply was returned.

Harvey's depressing dread was that his colored friend had heard the call and refused to reply. It might be he refrained through fear of the Professor, whom he held in abject awe, or possibly he was so obsessed by the trip to Africa that he was resolute not to allow any interference by his friends. Finally Harvey muttered:

"I don't believe he is within reach of my signals; it will be the fortune of Dick to bring him out from cover."

A possibility occurred to the young aviator. If Bunk had heard his call he would set out on a stealthy search for Harvey. He would steal like a red Indian through the undergrowth, around the rocks and among the tree trunks in the effort to gain a peep at the one who had followed him to his lonely retreat. Harvey stood motionless, listening and peering around for some minutes, and then, hearing nothing more than he had heard from the first, he started on a little search of his own.

Feeling the necessity of the utmost caution, he inched around to the rear of the ledge, halting at every step and peering into the labyrinth of undergrowth and tree trunks, many of which grew close to one another as if crowded for room. When he reached the spot he had in mind, a thrill ran through him, for he assuredly heard something moving apparently with the same care he was himself using. He stood motionless and listened.

The noise was so faint that for a time he could not tell the direction whence it came. He was in the midst of a dense growth of bushes, woven through in many places by matted vines which at times blocked his way.

"Bunk was always good at this business," he reflected; "I remember he used to trace me and Dick and dodge us when we were hunting for him. I don't believe he has detected me, but may suspect I am looking for him. Sh! there it is again."

This time he identified the point from which the indistinct rustling issued. It was to the left and perhaps a hundred feet away. The intervening growth made his view uncertain, but while gazing he saw some bushes agitated, as they might have been by a person stealing through them. He noticed that the very gentle breeze which was blowing came from the spot toward him, whereat he was glad, for he fancied his own movements were not so likely to be noticed by Bunk, provided it was really he who was so near.

Fearful of being discovered before he could get nigh enough to the colored youth to prevent his running off, Harvey took several guarded steps, which placed him behind the trunk of a large oak, and peered out.

The rustling ceased; then he heard it again and saw the bushes stirred. He thought this was a most peculiar way of acting on the part of his friend. After waiting until it had lasted several minutes without any change, he grew impatient. He stepped from behind the oak and advanced, keenly watching the bushes in front.

Suddenly an immense pair of antlers loomed to view amid the dense shrubbery and Harvey observed the head of a huge buck which was browsing upon a species of berry that grew on the upper part of a group of bushes. The direction of the wind prevented the animal from scenting the nearness of an enemy, but he had discovered something that roused his suspicion. He stopped chewing and holding his head high stared around in quest of the cause.

Harvey did not think of screening himself from sight of the buck, and immediately recalled the accounts Dick had written home of the huge creature for whose antlers he yearned.

"This must be the fellow; I don't suppose he would mind such a weapon as my revolver, even if it wasn't against the law to shoot his kind at this season, but Til give him a good scare for making me think he was Bunk."

With which the youth flung up his arms, uttered a loud "Whoof!" and bounded through the undergrowth toward the buck. Instead of making off in a panic, the animal looked for a moment at the approaching form, and then lowering his head charged straight at it.

This was turning the tables with a vengeance. Harvey Hamilton had set out to hunt a magnificent buck only to awake suddenly to the fact that the buck was hunting him.

"Jingo! I didn't expect that!" exclaimed our young friend, whirling round and dashing off at headlong speed.

"I wonder if he can climb a tree," was the next thought of the panic-stricken youth, who, without drawing the small weapon, which would have been practically useless, glanced hurriedly around for a refuge. He had precious little time to spare, for the brute was crashing down upon him like a runaway locomotive on a down grade.

A few paces away the fugitive thought he saw what he longed for, in the shape of a limb as thick as his arm, which put out at right angles from a trunk eight or ten feet above the ground. He could leap upward, catch hold and swing himself above the branch, but while running with might and main it suddenly occurred to him that the support was too low, and the towering antlers would overtake him before he could scramble out of their reach.

He heard the superb terror so close on his heels that, after running a few paces farther, he glanced over his shoulder to learn how many more seconds he had to live. As he did so, his foot caught in a wirelike vine which wound along the ground and he sprawled forward on his hands and knees.

Harvey not only fell but kept on falling. He had struck the edge of a ravine down which he shot so abruptly that he was gone beyond the power of checking himself, before he knew what was happening. He felt he was sinking and flung out his hands in a desperate effort to save himself, though he might well have questioned whether he was not fortunate after all in the promised escape from his infuriated pursuer. He gripped bush after bush, but in every instance it was uprooted and remained in his hands or gave way to others which he seized and which in their turn yielded to the strain. Then came the terrifying thought that the buck would tumble down upon him and crush out the breath of life.

Harvey was absolutely helpless. He might have been badly hurt by his fall had not his attempts to stop his descent so broken its force that when he suddenly landed on his feet he was only slightly jarred. In the same moment that this occurred, he plunged to one side so as to be out of the way of the avalanche which he expected from above.

But the buck was wiser in his way than the young aviator. Stillness followed the involuntary descent of the latter, and then the animal was heard threshing through the undergrowth. Whatever intentions he had held regarding the lad were given up and he went off.

"I wonder whether any fellow ever had a stranger escape," reflected Harvey, when he realized that he had nothing more to dread from the brute; "he would have had me sure but for that tumble."

The fear that the buck might be waiting in the vicinity held Harvey listening for some minutes. He was disturbed by the thought that his foe might find a path into the gorge and still have it out with him, but nothing of the kind occurred.

When finally he felt it safe to move about, he set out to learn his real situation, and the result was disquieting. His first thought was that the gap through which he had been precipitated was a ravine out of which he could climb with little difficulty; but to his dismay he found that it was a pocket or hole, which might be compared to an immense irregular well, twenty or thirty feet in diameter, with a depth nearly as great. The inclosing walls were of rock not only perpendicular but in several places the top narrowed, thus leaving the bottom broader than above. Only in one spot did the bushes grow to the edge, and that was where he had fallen, bringing so much undergrowth with him that he was not harmed.

Having made an inspection of his rocky prison, the all-important question presented itself: How was he to get out of it?

His hope was that by grasping the projecting bits of stone, he could climb to the upper edge, but the more he studied the problem the harder it seemed. There was one place where he finally decided to make the attempt. He believed he could raise himself to the top, but for the fact that about half way thither, the wall protruded in a way to suggest in a modified form the feat of treading a ceiling after the manner of a fly.

This slope, however, was so moderate and so short that he believed he might succeed. He was not encumbered with luggage and his outer coat had been left by the lakeside with the canoe and the fish which he and his brother had counted upon to furnish them their evening meal. The field glass being suspended by a cord behind his shoulders was no handicap; arms and legs were free to do their best, and few youths of his age were more capable athletes than he. The longer he studied the situation, the higher his hopes rose.

CHAPTER XV
A DISMAL NIGHT

BEFORE making an attempt to climb out of the flinty "pocket" Harvey Hamilton studied his situation again, weakly hoping he could discover a more favorable spot for the essay upon which so much depended.

"This must be more than a hole in the ground," he decided, "for if it weren't, it would be filled with water from the rains and melting snow."

His supposition was right. It would be more proper to speak of the trap in which he was caught as an expansion of a gorge. On one side a fissure reached from the bottom to the top, with a similar opening opposite. Peeping through these in turn, Harvey noted that the channel beyond widened to several feet. Thus a torrent of water rushing through the ravine from the higher level, would find an outlet on the other side of the expansion and in a miniature way the wonderfully picturesque "Gorge of the Aare" would be reproduced.

"Ah, if either was a little wider!" mourned Harvey, after vainly trying to wedge his body through the narrow openings; "it would be fun to follow the ravine to its outlet or to some spot where I could find a ladder up the side, but that can't be."

Thus far nothing in the nature of fear had disturbed the young aviator. Several hours of daylight remained and he was confident that by bestirring himself, or, if necessary, calling for help, he would be extricated from his vexatious situation. He came back to the place upon which he had fixed his hopes and girded himself for the effort.

"I could do it if it wasn't for that bulge," he said to himself, glancing aloft, "though the wall happens to be higher there than anywhere else."

Grasping a rocky projection with one hand, he found a resting place for his feet and pulled himself upward for ten or a dozen inches. Looking over either shoulder he had a partial view of his groping shoes which after awhile found a resting place, and then he made another hitch. This was comparatively easy work, and if it would only last he could climb out as readily as if ascending the stairs at home. But nature delights in irregularity, and when she built the steps in the side of the gorge she did not consult the convenience of anyone.

As has been stated the inward thrust of the wall began at about half the height from the bottom. The slope was so slight that it might have been overcome, had the projections occurred at the right intervals and had they been big enough to give a secure foot or handhold. With the utmost pains Harvey closed his fingers around the support, one in each hand and began groping with the toes of his shoes. He recalled the configuration over which he had passed, and succeeded in thrusting the front of his right shoe into a crevice, but was unable to find a rest for the other foot. Once the toe caught, but the instant he bore upon it the shoe slipped free and beat the air. The rattling fragments showed that he had struck a spot where the shale was too rotten to be depended upon.

At his waist a horizontal fissure had served for his hands. If he could lift his feet sufficiently to use it and gain another support above, it would be of vast help, but he must first secure an upper hold. Looking aloft he saw a ledge that he thought would answer.

"If it gives way or my hands slip I shall fall," he concluded, after studying the task, "but it's my only hope and here goes."

He bent his knees slightly and leaped upward. His calculation was made so nicely that he caught the projecting ledge, and had nearly worked his shoes into the lower opening, when the shale in his grasp broke as if it were a decayed limb, and unable to stay his descent, he dropped to the bottom of the gorge. The distance was not sufficient to harm him much, though he was considerably jarred.

"Confound it!" he exclaimed, chagrined and angered; "if I could have passed that spot I should have reached the top."

He wondered whether it was worth while to try it again, but decided there was no reason to expect success. Even if he could climb beyond the place of his mishap, new obstacles would check him.

"As it was, I fell as far as I care to tumble; that is about all I've been doing," he grimly added, "since that plaguy buck took a shy at me. If a fellow could only fall upward, there would be a chance for me."

For the first time since his slip he asked himself how this affair was to end. He was sure he had nothing to fear as to the final outcome.

"Dick will wait where he is, if he gets on the track of Bunk; he will signal me to go to him, and when I don't come, he will head this way. He knows the spot near enough to come within hail and the rest will be easy."

Once more his thoughts reverted to Bunk. While the fellow might keep out of his reach, so long as he believed Harvey was trying to prevent his trip with Professor Morgan, and while he undoubtedly would resent such interference, it would be far different when he learned that Harvey was in trouble. The dusky youth would abandon everything and rush to his rescue. None knew this better than Harvey Hamilton himself, and he wondered whether there was not some way of apprising Bunk of his dilemma.

"At any rate, it's worth trying," was the conclusion which he proceeded straightway to act upon.

Instead of whistling as he had done before, Harvey shouted the name of his friend and added in the loudest voice at his command the emphatic declaration that he was in a hole and wished Bunk to come and help him out. The appeal, if heard, was certain to bring results, but the truth forced itself upon the supplicant, that the voice of a person at the bottom of a well thirty feet or so in depth cannot be made to carry far. Bunk might be within two or three hundred yards and yet not hear him.

Harvey kept up his appeals until he grew hoarse, but without bringing the rescue for which he so ardently hoped. Help was beyond reach and he must depend upon other means to free himself from prison.

If you can imagine his situation, you will understand how hard it was for him to stay idle. To fold one's hands and wait for the assistance that is likely to be delayed for an indefinite time, is impossible for a lad in the vigor of health and strength. By this time he had formed the conviction that Bunk was nowhere near. It was the brother who had gone to the right spot to find him.

"From the way Bunk has acted all along he will fight shy of Dick; even if he doesn't know what his errand is, he will try to avoid meeting him. Besides, my brother won't know how to handle him, as I should in his place."

Having given up hope of climbing out of the gorge by the means already tried, Harvey inspected the other portions more minutely. He studied the path by which he had made his hasty descent when running from the buck. There was a luxuriant growth of shrubbery on the upper edge, through which he had fallen, bringing down several handfuls with him. The roots were so weak that they simply broke his fall without checking his downward course.

"I wonder whether I can get enough support to allow me to climb out there. A bush is within reach that looks as if it might hold. I'll try it."

By standing on tiptoe he grasped the top, upon which he began slowly pulling until he lifted himself clear. Then with the same patience he drew himself up several feet, when he had to let go and grip the bush above. This did not look so strong, but it held and he climbed two or three feet farther.

"I shall make it," he thought with a thrill of hope; "if the next will stand it and several after that, I shall get to the top."

But that was what did not take place. He had caught hold of the third support when it instantly came out by the roots, and he tumbled again, landing upon his back, though still without hurt, for the distance was slight.

The last attempt convinced Harvey that he was so securely trapped that he was utterly unable to help himself. Irksome as was the task he could do nothing but await the arrival of his brother.

Before his encounter with the buck, he had had a long tramp through the wilderness and he had toiled so hard to liberate himself, that he was tired in body. He sat down at the base of the bushes that had failed him and thought over the situation.

"If I had come into the mountains alone," he reflected with a shudder, "nothing but heaven could save me from starving to death. I can't get out and there isn't a bit of food or a drop of water within reach. If anything should happen to Dick, it will be the end of me. But what could happen to him?" he asked in a sharp effort to drive away the frightful thought. "He is looking for Bunk and will keep it up till night, when he'll set out to look for me. He knows where to come and won't be long about it."

Thus Harvey sat in melancholy reflection until the gathering gloom told him the day was drawing to a close and night was closing in. Despite his natural hopefulness, he could not fight off a depression of spirits, which after all was natural in the circumstances. He was alone in a vast solitude, no one could hear his calls for help, and Dick might hunt for hours without finding him.

With his nerves strained to the tensest point, Harvey suddenly heard something move in the bushes at the top of the wall and directly above his head. The suspicion that it might be a wild animal likely to tumble down upon him caused him to leave his place and station himself on the opposite side of the gorge, where he drew his revolver and stood ready to defend himself if attacked.

Something was certainly stirring above. He caught the rustling at intervals, with pauses that lasted so long that he believed the creature, whatever it might be, had left the spot. Suddenly it occurred to the youth that it might be his brother or some person.

"Hello up there!" he called; "is that you Dick, or Bunk?"

The fact that no reply was returned satisfied Harvey that it was neither of his friends. Hoping it might be a man, he added in the same distinct voice:

"I fell down here this afternoon and can't get out unless somebody gives me a lift."

Harvey heard the rustling again, but nothing more. It was some kind of a wild animal prowling in the vicinity.

"He may be looking for a meal and is trying to decide upon the best way of attacking me," added the youth, keeping a sharp watch, with his weapon tightly grasped.

A chill ran over him at the belief that he caught the glint of a pair of eyes peering through the dusk, but if so they were withdrawn, and the fact that he heard nothing more made him suspect he had been mistaken. His imagination was so wrought up that he saw things which did not exist.

By and by the all-pervading darkness shut out everything from sight. He could not discern the rugged margin of the gorge that had become so familiar to him. There was a growing chilliness in the air which would have made his extra coat welcome. He thought of gathering enough sticks to start a fire, but recalled that all the fuel within reach was green and it would be almost impossible to kindle it. Besides, though wild animals dread a too close contact with flames, he feared the light would attract some of them to the spot. Even if he could set a blaze going, he could not maintain it long, and then the turn of his enemies would come. Accordingly, he gave over all intention of trying to brighten up his sombre surroundings.

The bottom of the gorge was free from dampness, for rain had not fallen for a long time, and had the circumstances been different Harvey might have passed the night in comparative comfort. He could not bring himself to lie down, but assumed a sitting position with his back against the wall. He was opposite the spot down which he had tumbled. Somehow he felt that if danger came it would be from that point, and he intended to be prepared for it.

"There's no possibility of my falling asleep; I am too nervous. I don't understand what keeps Dick away," he added petulantly, for he had reached anything but a pleasant frame of mind, in which he conjured up many causes that might explain his brother's absence. Aside from the difficulty he was likely to find in bringing Bunk to terms, he himself might have met with accident. The fact that he carried a rifle was no guarantee against the very mishap that had befallen Harvey himself.

It would be hours before the moon rose and though the sky was clear and the orb was near the full, the foliage was too abundant to permit its light to reach him. In the hope that Dick might be moving about not far off, the imprisoned young aviator shouted his name at intervals. He ceased to call for Bunk, for he no longer felt any hope that he was in the neighborhood.

When a young man sits on the ground with his back against a support and in an easy posture, and is absolutely certain that he will stay wide awake until morning, such a belief is generally soon followed by profound slumber. Such was the case with Harvey Hamilton, who would have remained unconscious throughout the darkness had he not been roused in the most startling manner conceivable.

CHAPTER XVI
DICK IS TEMPTED

YOU will remember that Dick Hamilton was not only a sophomore in Yale University, but had attained his twenty-first year. He was warranted therefore in looking upon himself as a full-grown man, while in his mind his brother Harvey was only a "kid." He treated him as such, but was none the less fond of him. It need not be added that Dick had a strong affection for Bohunkus Johnson because of his simplicity, honesty, unfailing good nature and love for the two brothers. Consequently when the elder learned of the singular peril in which the colored lad had fallen through no fault of his own, he was as resolute as Harvey that he should be saved if the task was within the range of accomplishment.

But he took an impulsive man's view of the situation. He was impatient with the regard shown the crazy inventor, Professor Morgan, and what he looked upon as awe and fear on the part of Harvey.

"I'll end this monkey business when I gain the chance," he reflected, after parting from his brother on the shore of the lake. "Let me once get within reach of Bunk and I'll yank him back to common sense quicker than he can say Jack Robinson. If he objects, I'll wipe the ground with him, and if Harv makes a kick I'll serve him the same way. As for the lunatic, if he can't be bluffed I'll use other means. He ought to be jugged where he can't get a chance to run off with such numskulls as Bunk. All I want is a show."

Which it may be said was all that Harvey wanted. Dick was confident that if he could once reach the colored lad all trouble would be over. But that was the crux of the situation: Bunk had not yet been found.

The elder Hamilton was sure that he was on his way to where the colored youth was a prisoner. And it was because of that confidence that he sent Harvey on his wild-goose chase.

"He won't get near Bunk. If he does, the wild man may drop down on both and raise the dickens with them. I should like to see him try it with me. I told Harv that I knew the section where I had seen him come down in his monoplane more than once, but I didn't tell him that I know pretty nearly the exact spot. If the court knows herself and she thinks she do, that spot is whither my footsteps are now tending."

It came about that the paths pursued by the brothers diverged more than the younger suspected. Instead of leading to points a fourth of a mile apart, the distance between them was fully double that.

"Now I shouldn't mind if the Professor arrived just behind me and tried to butt in. If he does I'll make things lively for him. I haven't had any special exercise since my boxing bout with big Burt Thompson and I should like to have a little fun with a full-grown man."

From which it will appear that the elder Hamilton held views which, to say the least, would have surprised his brother.

To Dick all seemed plain sailing, but such did not prove the fact. Having his destination clearly in mind he went straight to it. The place was similar in several respects to that visited by Harvey; but after a little search among the rocks, he came upon a cavern, which extended twenty feet back, with half that width and height, and the entire front open. It would serve well as a shelter during a storm but a fire would become necessary in cold weather.

One comprehensive glance showed that some one had occupied this primitive retreat during the past few days. The flinty floor was strewn with bones, bits of dry bread, pieces of paper that had evidently served for wrapping, bottles, and other debris which suggested that a party of picnickers had recently made use of it. At the rear was a single rumpled blanket that no doubt had served for a bed.

"This is Bunk's home," was the conclusion of the visitor, after his survey. "The Professor has warned him not to wander off, and keeps him supplied with the necessaries of life, which, knowing Bunk's appetite as I do, is no small job."

So much being conceded, Dick looked around for the occupant, satisfied that he must be near. Not seeing him, he raised his voice, as his brother did some time later at the other place.

"Come here, Bunk!" he called; "come a-running too, for if you don't I'll lambaste you out of your three and a half senses!"

When the summons had been repeated several times without results it occurred to Dick that he had been somewhat hasty. Gentler means might have prevailed. He decided that it might be well to appeal to the affectionate side of Bunk's nature, by calling out that Mr. and Mrs. Hartley were dead, that Harvey had fallen down stairs and broken his neck, and that Dick himself was not feeling well; but he decided to retain this stupendous bluff as a last reserve.

"He can't be far off," continued the young man, fast losing patience. Enough light entered the cavern from the front to show the interior clearly, but to make sure, he jerked the blanket from the stone floor and peeped under it, where a mouse would not have found room to hide itself. Then he strode outside and glanced sharply toward the different points of the compass.

"I'll shake him till his teeth rattle for doing this," muttered Dick; "I believe he is watching me all the time."

The conviction forced itself upon Dick Hamilton stronger than ever that he had taken a wrong method of dealing with the African youth. He ought to have waited until the fellow was within reach before being so emphatic. Bunk must have detected the approach of his old friend and hidden himself. The chances of doing this successfully were so numerous that it was useless for Dick to hunt for him. He must decide upon his next step.

He would have shouted out the fiction of misfortune having overtaken Harvey, thus appealing to the friendship of Bunk, had he not believed it was too late to adopt the subterfuge. The colored lad would see through the trick.

The only recourse that occurred to Dick was to pretend he had given up the search and go away as if to return to camp. He therefore called:

"Good bye, Bunk; when you get back from Africa you must tell us about your trip. I wish you good luck."

There was no response and he did not expect any. He picked his way through the undergrowth and among the trees and rocks, heading toward the lake, but soon changed his course with the purpose of joining Harvey a half mile distant. He would have preferred to notify him of his approach by whistling, but the signal most likely would have been heard by Bunk and would put him on his guard.

"I can reach Harv without trouble and he and I will fix upon a plan."

The young man was so impatient with Bunk that he longed for the chance to punish him for his foolishness.

"He holds that Professor in deadly fear, and is more afraid of offending him than of vexing us. I can understand how such a crank with his wild, magnetic eyes can gain a hypnotic power over the simple fellow, but he ought to throw off the spell when he knows the man is a long distance away and we are near him."

The route was so rough that Dick, who did not hurry, spent a long time in traversing it. He had gone the greater part of the way when a threshing in the underwood in advance brought him to an abrupt halt. He sprang behind the nearest tree and held his Winchester ready for use. He knew from the peculiar racket that an animal of some kind was approaching. As in the case of his brother, the gentle breeze was in his favor and the brute as yet was unaware of his presence.

"Well, I'll be hanged!"

The very buck about which he had written home in glowing terms, and which he had seen several times in the neighborhood, was stalking through the brush like a forest monarch, his course such that unless alarmed, he must pass within a few paces of the young hunter.

The temptation to bag the prize was almost resistless. Dick had only to reach out his hand, as may be said, to seize the treasure. With the deadly weapon in his grasp and many shots at command, he could drop the gigantic animal in his tracks. It would be easy to remove the magnificent antlers, hide them among the rocks, and return for them weeks later when the season was open. After that he would fill his classmates with rank unbearable jealousy.

It was natural perhaps that Dick Hamilton should fall back upon the specious reasoning which comes to him who meditates breaking the law. How can it be right to shoot an elk or deer on the sixteenth of September, and wrong to do so on the fifteenth? Can the simple wording of a statute decide the question? Of course not. Besides, none of the game protectors were near and at the most Dick would be compelled only to pay a big fine, for which the accommodating "governor" would readily stand.

It has been said that, as to the question of free moral agency, a logician may argue so subtly as to convince his hearers that such a thing is impossible. And yet there always remains one person whom he cannot convince, and that person is himself. So it came about that Dick's conscience would not down. He could not hush the still small voice.

Twenty yards away the buck was warned by his strange instinct that danger was in the air. He came to a halt, his big brown body only partially disclosed among the foliage, but when he reared his head, that and the glorious crown of curving prongs rose in relief against the emerald background. It was an ideal target and Dick Hamilton in a tremor brought his rifle to his shoulder. Slight as was the movement and imperceptible the noise, the buck wheeled and fled on the instant. Just then the youth should have pressed the trigger, but instead he lowered his weapon.

"I can't do it!" he said, compressing his lips; "it isn't out of mercy for you, my fine fellow, but because the law says 'No!'"

It will be understood that the buck had finished with the younger brother, who escaped his knife-like hoofs through accident. The query naturally occurs as to why the creature should run toward one youth and away from the other. Ask any veteran or amateur hunter, and he will answer that it was because in one case the biped had a deadly weapon and in the other he had not. It sounds absurd, but you can never make a ranger of the woods believe that the game animals do not govern their actions in accordance with the open and close seasons.

"I must be real good," said Dick Hamilton airily as he resumed his tramp, "thus to crush my fondest hopes and dash away the tempting cup held to my lips, but all the same, I almost wish I had dropped that fellow."

By this time he was so much nearer Harvey than to Bohunkus that Dick emitted the signal to which all were accustomed. He hardly expected a reply and did not receive any, the singular situation being that at that very moment the brothers were issuing their calls and yet neither could hear the other. Harvey's location at the bottom of the gorge shut in his voice and signals and shut out those of Dick. Had the former been standing above the gorge where only trees and brush intervened, the two would have come together in a brief while.

Despite the assurance of Dick, he wandered from the course he intended to follow. It will be remembered that the region was strange to him and he had no guiding landmarks. When he awoke to the unpleasant fact night was closing in. He did not know what direction to take to reach Harvey and signaled repeatedly, but inasmuch as he was a good deal farther off than in the first place, it need not be said that his calls failed to reach the ears for which they were meant. He strove to regain his bearings, and since he was able to locate the lake and saw the glimmer of the camp fire beyond, he accomplished much in the way of correcting his course.

"I wonder whether anything has happened to Harv," he mused, with a vague uneasiness stealing over him; "I don't see what could have harmed him, for he has his Colt and no animals in this part of the world will attack a fellow in his situation. He is too used to tramping through the woods to fall over the rocks or to tumble into any chasm."

Little did the elder brother suspect how near he had hit upon the truth.

Satisfied that he was on the right course, Dick pressed on until the darkness became too deep for him to see his way. He halted and peered around in the starlight, but his vision was too obstructed to give any satisfaction.

"As nearly as I can figure out I am pretty near the spot. If I am right, why in the mischief doesn't he answer me?"

He raised his voice once more and shouted and whistled. In this instance Harvey would have made reply but for the fact that he was asleep. All through the racket he slumbered as serenely as if in his own bed at home.

Dick, with his hands extended in front, one grasping his Winchester, groped forward, careful where he placed each foot in turn.

"I can't say that I fancy this work. If I don't bump against Harv pretty soon I'll give it up for the night.

"What the deuce—" he abruptly exclaimed as he felt himself sinking downward.

CHAPTER XVII
AN UNCEREMONIOUS ARRIVAL

BY a remarkable coincidence Dick Hamilton trod in the very steps of his brother Harvey while groping about the gorge, and went crashing and tumbling to the bottom in the precise fashion of his predecessor.

Retaining his grasp on his Winchester, he strove desperately to check his descent, but from the causes mentioned failed and landed on his feet, bewildered and unable for the moment to comprehend what had taken place. The racket and his exclamations roused Harvey, who was so mystified that he whipped out his revolver and fired a shot in the direction of the noise without being able to discern his target.

"Stop that!" shouted the elder; "you may hit me!"

"Heavens, Dick, is it you?" demanded the younger.

Finding himself unharmed, Dick's waggery asserted itself.

"I don't know who else it is. That's the way I always come downstairs. What are you doing here?"

"Waiting to welcome you."

"A pretty way to receive a long lost brother by shooting at him."

"I didn't harm you, did I?"

"Of course not, for you aimed at me."

"How could I do that when I didn't see you?"

"All the same in both cases. But I say, Harv, what does all this mean? It's the queerest mix up I ever ran into."

"The same with me; I tumbled down that bank while picking my way along the edge."

"You see the effect of a bad example. How long have you been here?"

"It seems about a month, but I guess it is only a few hours."

"Why didn't you answer my signals?"

"For the same reason that you didn't answer mine."

"But I was so near when I last called that you ought to have heard me."

"So I should if I hadn't been asleep. You woke me rather suddenly."

"Couldn't help it; you might have put up a notice warning me to look out. But I say, Harv, what sort of a hotel is this?"

"One that I should like very much to leave."

"Why haven't you done so?"

"Couldn't; I wish you would show me the way out."

"Take the first door you come to."

"But there isn't any door; I tried to bid farewell until I had to give it up."

Harvey now told the particulars of his mishap. The gloom was so deep that neither could see even the outlines of the other. But their hands met and both were thankful over their escape, though their situation was anything but enviable. Dick drew out his match safe and held the tiny flame above his head. As the reflection lighted each face, they laughed.

"We set out to find Bunk," said the elder, "and now it's up to him to find us. You say you know of no way of climbing out of this gorge?"

"Not unless some one gives us help. I have tried it over and over again, and shouted until I was hoarse, but without any one hearing me."

"I certainly did not. Now instead of one young Hamilton in a hole there are two. That makes the situation twice as bad as before. Why haven't you started a fire?"

"The fuel is too green."

"Thereby resembling us. However, we must find some way to leave in the morning. You see, Harv, we haven't our outer coats, nor any food, nor moisture enough to wet our lips. By and by our situation will become a bore."

"It is pretty near that now."

Since it was certain they would have to spend the night there, they seated themselves where Harvey had been resting when awakened with such startling suddenness.

"Did you learn anything of Bunk?" asked Dick.

"I didn't get the first trace."

"I knew you wouldn't when you left me."

"How did you make out?"

"I found the cave where he was staying and had a talk with him."

"What!" exclaimed the amazed Harvey; "do you tell me that?"

"I suppose it is hardly fair to say I had a talk with him, being that I did all the talking and he hadn't a word to reply."

"Why not?"

"Fact is I didn't lay eyes on him; he kept out of sight."

Thereupon the elder related his experience after the two had parted company. There was no doubt that he had come upon the temporary dwelling of the missing Bohunkus, but the fellow eluded him.

"We'll have him yet," added Dick, "and if I feel then as I do now, I'll teach him a lesson he won't forget if he lives a thousand years."

"Perhaps he deserves it, though I don't blame him as much as you do."

"I am speaking for myself, and I'll drop a hint to you that it won't be prudent to interfere. I may be in a different mood when I reach him."

"Remember, you haven't reached him as yet and there's no saying when you will."

"I haven't any doubt that the morning will show us so easy a way of getting out of this hole, that you'll be disgusted because you didn't see it at once."

Dick's optimism cheered Harvey. They talked for two hours and then both succumbed to drowsiness. They adjusted their positions so as to bring a part of their bodies in contact, thus gaining a slight degree of mutual warmth. While the night continued cool they did not suffer, and the slumber into which they sank lasted without break until morning.

Dick was the first to regain his senses. Gently moving so as not to disturb his brother he made a minute inspection of the gorge, passing twice around it, and studying every spot upon which it seemed possible to build hope. He was scrutinizing the inward sloping wall overhead which Harvey had tried to climb when the latter, still seated, looked up.

"Well, what do you make of it?"

"I must own that it looks dubious. I don't see any way of getting to the top. I thought of raising you on my shoulders but that wouldn't amount to anything."

"It will do no good to whistle or shout, for no one, unless near, can hear us. How long before Hunter and Wadsworth will suspect something is wrong and set out to hunt you up?"

"They will probably wait for one or two weeks, by which time we should be somewhat hungrier and thirstier than now, though that doesn't seem possible. Then," grimly added Dick, "if they come to this spot they would probably tumble into the gorge the same as we did, and we should all have to die together. I have a plan that may possibly amount to something."

Dick took his Winchester from where it leaned against the rocks, and pointing the muzzle toward the sky, discharged each of the ten charges with a few seconds between them. Then he refilled the chamber with cartridges and waiting a few minutes, did as before.

"Those reports will carry farther than our whistling or shouting, but not as far as I should like. It depends upon whether anyone is in the neighborhood."

The experiment proved delightfully successful. Dick Hamilton was preparing to fire a third series, when they were thrilled by a shout:

"Hello, down there! What the blazes is the matter?"

The hail came from a point behind them. On the edge of the gorge and close to where the brothers had fallen one after the other, stood a middle-aged man in rough clothing and a slouch hat, carrying a rifle. His face was smooth-shaven, and the expression kindly.

"Look out!" Harvey shouted, "or you'll fall into the gorge."

"I reckon I ain't fool enough to do that," was his grinning reply; "is that the way you managed it?"

"That's what we did," said Dick; "be good enough not to laugh too hard, for we feel bad enough as it is, without your rubbing it in."

"You do seem to be in a fix, but we can soon get you out."

"You have no surer way of earning our undying gratitude," said Dick.

"Wait where you be till I come back."

"There's no fear of not waiting, but please don't forget to return."

"Don't be afraid."

With which the man drew back and disappeared. He was not gone long when he reappeared with a long, slim sapling, which he had trimmed of its nubs and excrescences except at the top. Bracing himself firmly on another part of the edge of the gorge, which was the lowest and gave firm footing, he grasped the larger end of the pole and carefully thrust the smaller part down into the opening.

"Can you make it?" he called, peering over.

By standing on tiptoe Dick could grasp the bushy end. He suggested that Harvey should go first, but there was really no choice, and the younger replied by telling his brother not to wait.

"Are you ready?" asked the man above.

"Hold fast and I'll climb up. You needn't lift me."

It was easy for the elder, even with his rifle in one hand, to ascend the pole monkey fashion, and a minute later he stood on the upper ground beside his friend. Then he helped to hold the larger end and Harvey climbed up with the same facility. The rescue was effected so readily that it was almost ridiculous. The two warmly thanked the stranger. Harvey offered a money reward, but the man shook his head.

"I'm Jim Haley, one of the game protectors for this part of the country. I heard your gun and wondered what it meant. We have to keep sharp watch of them as are inclined to forget this is the close season. Why have you brought your Winchester with you?" asked the official, with a suspicious look at Dick.

"I generally carry it in the woods so as to be ready for danger. I met a big buck yesterday; fact is, I've seen him several times and he was mighty tempting, but I haven't any wish to get into trouble with the courts."

"Don't forget that, young man, for if you do it'll go hard with you."

"I'll remember," meekly replied Dick, who almost trembled to recall how near he had come to violating the game laws; "a couple of friends and myself have a tent on the other side of the lake. If you will go there with us I can promise you a good breakfast and a smoke."

Haley thanked them but declined the invitation, and bidding them good day strode off. His manner showed that he was still a little distrustful of the intentions of the young man, who, it need hardly be said, gave him and his brother officials no further cause to suspect him.

"The next thing to be done," said Dick, "is to get back to camp for breakfast. On the way we'll stop long enough to lower the lake six inches in slaking our thirst."

"What about Bunk?" asked Harvey.

"On his account, I shall give him no attention till after I have had a full meal. If I should run across him before, nothing can prevent me from murdering him."

"We have a fine mess of fish awaiting us at the canoe."

"But nothing else; we need seasoning, coffee, biscuit and lots of other things that can't be had short of camp. I'll run you a race."

"Not if I know myself."

So it came about that Bohunkus Johnson was dismissed from their thoughts for the time, and all their energies were given to making the trip as quickly as possible. Dick plied the paddle with skill and vigor. They found their friends awaiting them and the meal which followed was all that two hungry youths could ask.

While it was under way, Hunter and Wadsworth having concluded theirs, the Hamiltons told their story. The morning was now well advanced and Professor Morgan and his monoplane might appear at any moment. The couple, who were making ready for a tramp in the woods to the eastward, volunteered to go with Dick and Harvey, but it was feared that their presence might prove an obstacle to success.

"We are starting for that sable gentleman in earnest this time," said the elder, "and what's more, we're going to get him. You can bet your last dollar on that. I've got a hunch to that effect."

"You are likely to run into a row with the Professor," said Hunter.

"Nothing would suit me better; I have had so much experience while in camp in dealing with cranks that I understand 'em."

With good wishes the parties separated as on the day before, and once more Dick Hamilton sent the canoe skimming toward the extremity of the lake He would not permit Harvey to take the paddle, for he was less skillful. The minutes were important.

"Keep watch for that lunatic, Harv, and leave the rest to me."

The younger not only scanned the sky to the south, but studied the mountainous country ahead. The greater part of the distance had been passed when he uttered an excited exclamation.

"What is it?" asked Dick, holding his paddle suspended and glancing over his shoulder.

"Take a look at that pile of rocks where you went yesterday and let me know what you see."

Dick laid down the paddle and leveled the instrument. A moment later he called out:

"I'll be hanged! It's Bunk and no mistake!"

CHAPTER XVIII
BUNK JOINS THE PROFESSOR

I FEAR that our glimpses of Bohunkus Johnson have been so vague that you think it is time something more positive should be told. Let us therefore give our attention to the colored youth and make clear what befell him. It becomes necessary to go back to that day in eastern Pennsylvania when he parted company with Harvey Hamilton. His extraordinary experience was wholly due to the little tiff he had had with the young aviator. How true it is that "great oaks from little acorns grow." But for that trifling affair I should have finished my story long ago.

It is a hard thing to deal with a brilliant mind gone askew, especially when the line between sanity and insanity becomes at times indistinct, if it does not wholly disappear. Professor Milo Morgan was carried away by his intense interest in aeronautics. You have learned of the remarkable inventions he had already made in that field. He had discovered how to make the flight of his machine noiseless, and could remain in the air for ten or twelve hours. Not only that, but he had succeeded in constructing a helicopter,—that is, an aeroplane that will rise vertically by means of the horizontal screw or propeller beneath.

Having achieved all this, he became absorbed in the scheme of remaining aloft for two days at least. When he could do that he would be able, while traveling at the rate of seventy-five miles an hour, to cross the Atlantic between Quebec and Liverpool (2600 miles) in a trifle less than a day and a half. That his ambition was not so mad as it may seem, I may add that, while I am writing these lines, a professional aviator has declared that he is certain of accomplishing the feat in the near future. I venture to predict, that within the next three years the trip will be made by more than one aviator.

The Professor was so rapt in his work that he thought of nothing else and became indifferent toward every one. He cared nothing for Harvey or Bunk or the great task of Detective Pendar. What he did by way of aiding them may be called side issues. The chances came in his way and he used them as he might have used a score of others of a different nature, with no thought or interest or care in what should follow.

When the African youth came to him at the hotel in Chesterton and asked the privilege of accompanying him to Africa, the proposal was promptly accepted. It may have been that the crank took a liking to the big, honest fellow, but it is more probable he saw that Bohunkus would become more than a simple passenger. The man had felt the need of an assistant, — not a negative person, but one who could help him in what might be called the rough work he had in hand. It was physical, not mental aid that he wanted while engaged in completing his experiments with full success in sight.

The Professor inquired whether Bunk was at liberty to go with him on the long aerial voyage. In other words must he have the permission of young Hamilton?

"Huh!" sniffed the lad, in whose heart still rankled resentment because of his late rebuke; "he hain't got nuffin to do with me; I'm my own boss and he knows better dan to put on airs with me."

"That being the case I will take you, but it will be two or three days before I shall be ready to start."

"Dat don' make no diff'rence, so you starts some time. I can wait, I reckons, till yo' am suited."

"And you may have some hard work to perform in helping me."

"I'm used to work; dat don't scare me; jes' tell me what yo' want done and I'll doot."

"I recall something about your father being a great chief in Africa."

"Dat's de fac'," replied Bunk proudly; "he am de greatest chief in de whole state; he'll treat yo' mighty well for fetching me ober to wisit him."

How Bohunkus first gained the belief that his parent belonged to the native nobility of the Dark Continent is interesting of itself. When he was very small he was brought to Mr. Cecil Hartley, the well-to-do farmer who was a neighbor of Mr. Hamilton near Mootsport, by an aged negro who had been a slave in the South. He said the father of the urchin was the great chief Bohunkus Foozleum, who was at the head of a clan numbering thousands of warriors in Central Africa. The old man added that the Christian name of Bunk was Johnson, which, if a fact, is rather hard to understand. However, Bunk was turned over to the kind-hearted farmer and his wife, and was known as a bound boy, though the transfer was not accompanied by the usual legal steps.

The yarn of the old negro was repeated many times in the hearing of Bunk, and the Hartleys and Hamiltons often laughed over it. The gravity they assumed when telling the story to Bunk naturally caused him to believe it, and again naturally he formed the resolution that whenever a chance offered he would visit that hazy country and make a call upon his royal parent.

Hence his quickness to seize what looked like a golden opportunity.

"You must understand one thing from the start," said the Professor impressively.

"Yas, sir."

"If you enter my service there will be no turning back,—you must go with me to the end."

"Dat soots me from de sole ob my head to de crown ob my foot. I doan' keer if I neber come back; being chief among dem folks am a good deal better dan being lambasted and aboosed by white folks."

"How long will it take you to get ready?"

"'Bout four seconds; all I've got to git am my coat and a few little tings dat am in my room up-stairs."

"Get them then."

Bunk sprang to his feet and was hurrying through the door of the hotel when the Professor called him back.

"You mustn't tell anyone of this, especially young Hamilton."

"How am I gwine to tell him when he ain't here to tell? We'll be half way to Afriky afore he comes back."

"You mustn't write any letter and leave it here for him."

"Neber thought ob doing dat," replied Bunk, as he dived from sight and went up the stairs three steps at a time.

It was just there that Professor Morgan made his first mistake. It was true, as Bunk said, that he had no thought of leaving any message for his young friend, but since he had been forbidden to do so, the temptation to disobey was irresistible. Temporary resentment could not quench his affection for Harvey Hamilton.

"When he comes back and finds me gone, he'll cry his eyes out; he'll butt his head agin de wall and call on de hotel to fall down and mash him flat. Harv ain't such a bad feller as some folks think."

The result of all this was that Bunk wrote his farewell epistle in his room and had no trouble in handing it to the landlord who, as we know, carried out his wishes.

Now that the decision had been made, the colored youth was all eagerness to start. He was in mortal fear that Harvey would return at any moment. While Bunk was as resolute as ever he did not wish to come to an open quarrel with Harvey Hamilton.

Not once did a thought enter his mind that the aviator's brain was muddled. He looked upon the strange person with awe and fear. While he might disregard instructions when the eye of his master was not upon him, nothing could have made him do so otherwise. The Professor's hypnotic power was complete. By fixing those piercing orbs upon the negro, he could readily cast over him that strange spell which we have all seen and which made the youth as putty in his hands. The man did not call this ability into play, because the need had not as yet appeared, but he knew it was at his command whenever he wished to use it.

"We're off for Afriky!" was the thrilling thought of Bunk, when he sat back in his seat and with swelling heart looked out into the radiant sky and the variegated landscape sweeping under him. Never was he so proud and never did his heart swell with such abounding emotion.

"Won't Harv feel sorry when he sees me coming back from my visit to the great chief dat has de honor of being my fader? I'll catch de biggest elephant in Afriky as I promised Harv and hang him to de bottom of dis machine so dat his legs will swing clear and he can see de country below him. I can make room fur de giraf in dis seat alongside ob me, and let his head stick frough de top where he can obsarbe eberyting in front and back and at de side, and above and below. Gee! how he'll enjoy it.

"Chief Foozleum must be mighty rich. I'll git him to gib me two or free bushels ob diamonds and sew 'em all ober my clothes and hab a big one on de end ob each foot."

There was no end to the extravagant fancies that roved through the brain of Bohunkus. He looked at that strange figure in front, always sitting bolt upright with a hand loosely grasping a lever on each side, while he stared straight ahead as if trying to peer beyond the range of ordinary vision. For long intervals Bunk could not see the slightest movement of limb or head. The linen duster was buttoned closely about the gaunt form and as he sat on the lower end of the garment the keen wind did not cause any flapping. By and by there would be a slight twitch of one of the levers and a change in direction would follow, though otherwise it would not have been noticeable. Since the air was calm, a keen breeze was produced by the progress of the helicopter, which was traveling fully a mile a minute. Bunk had donned his heavy coat before starting and was glad he did so, for he had to rub his ears to keep them warm.

As was his custom the aviator flew low, sometimes approaching within a hundred feet of the tops of the trees or the tall buildings in the towns over which he skimmed. Bunk was startled once or twice by fear of a collision, but the Professor was not only a marvelous expert, but his machine responded with quick sensitiveness. At the slightest move of hand or foot it would turn to one side, dart upward or dive downward, as he willed. After a time Bunk's misgiving left him and his confidence in the man became perfect.

The aerial voyage to the southern Adirondacks was so similar in most respects to what has been described that we need not dwell upon it. The Professor did not stop on the way, and when he reached his workshop the fluid in the tank would have taken him back without halt to his starting point. He believed he could keep aloft with undiminished speed for twenty hours if not longer, but it would not answer to head eastward over the Atlantic until able to do better than that. He had set the limit at two days, for he was wise enough to give himself a fair margin. It might become necessary to reduce his speed when over mid-ocean, or some slight disarrangement of his machinery was possible, though of the latter he felt little fear.

Upon the arrival of the couple at the workshop, Bunk was pleased to do his first work for his master. He was told to run the monoplane into the hangar which stood to one side and slightly to the rear of the more important structure. He performed the task so deftly that the Professor complimented him.

"I see that you may become quite valuable to me," said he in his sepulchral voice, after he had opened the door of the cabin and peeped in. "Sit down on those steps while I have a few words with you."

"Yas, sir," responded Bunk as he obeyed him.

"How much wages do you think you ought to receive, Bohunkus?"

"Bress yo' heart, Perfesser, I doan' want no wages for what I does for yo'; ain't yo' gwine to take me 'cross de Pacific Ocean?"

"Not the Pacific,—the Atlantic."

"Dat's what I meant; yo's gwine to do a good deal moah fur me dan I am fur yo'."

"I don't wish anyone to work for me without pay; suppose I give you ten dollars a week and your keep."

Bunk airily waved his hand and replied:

"Doan' make no difference to me; if yo's gwine to feel bad I'll take it, but," he added with an inspiring thought, "it am on two conditions."

"What are they?"

"Dat when we calls on Chief Foozleum I shall gib you a pocket full ob diamonds so as to make it squar'."

"I have no objection to that; what is the other condition?"

"Dat yo' gib me plenty to eat."

For the first and only time in his life, Bunk saw the grizzled whiskers at the side of the Professor's mouth twitch in a way that showed he was smiling. It was only for an instant, however, when he was as grave as before.

"Your terms are reasonable. I had forgotten about it's being meal time."

"I hadn't," said Bunk with a sigh.

"You may have noticed that we have landed not far from a town; it's name is Dawson; I am acquainted with the landlord and will go there for supper. I shall bring back a good meal for you."

"Ain't yo' gwine to take me along?" asked the surprised Bunk; "I can carry de food a good deal better inside ob me dan yo' can outside ob yo'self."

"I prefer that it should not be known for the present that you are with me; I'll walk to the hotel and I promise you not to keep you waiting long."

A few minutes later the Professor took his departure and did as he had agreed.

CHAPTER XIX
IN THE WORKSHOP

THAT night the Professor forgot the existence of Bohunkus Johnson and indeed of everything in the world except the absorbing task before him. He threw his workshop into one dazzling, overwhelming blaze and began labor at once. The structure of his machine was perfected: all that remained was to force nature to yield her secret by which the fuel of the aeroplane could be held effective for two days of twenty-four hours each. He was sure he was on the verge of the marvelous discovery.

Before delving into his fascinating work he instructed Bunk as to how he should dispose of himself. The boy had eaten a bountiful meal and though the hour was early was drowsy.

"You can hear the ripple of the small stream at the rear of the hangar; there you can drink or bathe night or morning; here are your sleeping quarters."

He pointed to the rear of the shop where lay a plank covered with a single blanket. It was the custom of the Professor to stretch himself upon this when he felt the need of rest, which it may be said was infrequently. He did not expect to sleep on this night, but if compelled to do so, would snatch brief repose by half reclining in a rustic chair which stood back of the door at the front. By and by, Bunk's head began to nod, and bidding the Professor good night he made his way uncertainly to his couch. Just then the man's foot was on the treadle and he was pressing some kind of instrument against the whizzing face of a tiny stone wheel. He made no response to the salutation of his assistant and probably did not hear him.

Bunk lay on his side so as to watch the aviator at his work. He saw him flit from one side of the shop to the other and mix several kinds of liquid, one of which gave out so pungent an odor that the youth sneezed, but without attracting the attention of the experimenter. Then followed a series of vivid flashes in which all the colors of the spectrum blinded the awed spectator. The man filed, cut, scraped, compounded, and did no end of things until Bunk grew weary and glided into dreamland.

He must have slept well beyond midnight, when apparently without cause he awoke. For a few minutes he was too confused to locate himself. Gradually his recollection came back, and he realized that he was in blank darkness. His immediate surroundings were so still that he heard the soft ripple of the brook near the hangar.

"I 'spose de Perfesser hab retired," concluded Bunk, "and I shan't see anything ob him till morning."

It was so easy, as a rule, for the colored youth to sleep at all times that he could not understand why he not only awoke from sound slumber but could not woo it back. The longer he lay the wider awake he became. Finally he sat up.

"Dis am mighty qu'ar," he muttered; "it looks as if morning hab come afore de night am frough; I wonder if tings doan' got mixed dat way sometimes in dis part ob de world."

The question was beyond his solving. His next feeling was of curiosity as to the whereabouts of the Professor. When Bunk last saw him he was working in the vividly lighted shop. By and by the lad made out a faint illumination through the windows that was caused by the partially obscured moonlight. The door was shut, since nothing of the kind showed in that direction.

"I'll bet dat he's goned off," was Bunk's decision; "I wonder if he means to gib me de slip and sail to Afriky without me. I'll find out."

He recalled the interior of the building well enough to remember that a wide passage led from his couch to the opening at the front. The workbenches were along the sides, so as to give the inventor elbowroom. Bunk began groping his way with hands extended to avoid falling over any obstacle that might have been placed there while he was asleep. His wakefulness was probably due to the effect of the fumes of chemicals, for he had noted them the moment he roused from slumber.

"I'll go outside and if I doan' see de Perfesser I'll yell for him —"

Bunk did not wait until he got outside before yelling. At that moment, one of his extended hands came in contact with a live, or rather partly live wire, and with a wild shout he bounded several feet in air, tumbled over on his back, kicked and rolled in an agony more of mind than of body. In the same instant, the interior of the building was illuminated as if from the burst of a hundred suns. As his bewildered senses straggled back he rose to a sitting posture and saw the towering form of Professor Morgan looking down upon him with the most terrible expression he had ever witnessed on his countenance. Like the youth, he had not removed his garments and the long duster still wrapped his towering figure. The eyes glowed with piercing intensity and Bunk even fancied that the long grizzled beard was in flames.

"What is the matter with you?" sternly demanded the crank, in the voice which sounded like the rolling of thunder.

"I guess I'm killed," replied the bewildered Bunk, slowly climbing to his feet, "or mebbe it were a mule dat kicked me. Hab yo' got a mule round here?"

"Fool!" exclaimed the Professor angrily, "didn't you know better than to go groping round the shop in the darkness? It is a miracle that you were not killed by a thousand volts; why didn't you call me?"

"I didn't see yo' nowhere 'bout; 'scuse me."

"If you had called I should have heard you. I was asleep like yourself."

"I didn't hear yo' breeving; I say, Perfesser," added Bunk with more boldness than he had yet dared to show, "ain't yo' keerless in leaving dem blue blazes layin' 'round where dey am likely to swipe a feller in de face when he ain't doing nuffin?"

"You surely will be killed if you go nosing round the shop when I'm not with you."

"Yo' war wid me but I didn't know it. I say, Perfesser, wouldn't yo' as lieb move to some oder place?"

The inventor in front of the trembling Bunk still looked keenly at him, as if a new thought had flashed into his brain. He spoke with more kindness than he had shown since they had been together:

"Bohunkus, I'm satisfied that this isn't the place for you, though I shall have to stay myself until we are ready to start. To-morrow I shall take you to new quarters."

"Dat am de best news I've heerd in sebenteen years; dere's only one thing dat would soot me better."

"What is that?"

"To hear yo' say dat we's gwine to start to Afriky."

"Be patient for a day or two. Now, wouldn't you like to go back to your home at Mootsport and stay there?"

Bunk did not suspect this was a test question and was honest in his answer:

"No, sah; not till we've been to Afriky and spent a few weeks wid Chief Foozleum."

"You wouldn't leave me if I gave you the chance?"

"Not fur de world; do yo' think I wanter to go home and hear Harv and Dick Hamilton and dere folks laugh at me? Not much."

"Suppose they come after you?"

"Dat's nuffin; I'm my own boss; dey wouldn't git me by a jugful."

"I shall see that they don't while I am present," said the Professor with a glint of his fiery eyes; "I'll attend to that, but I shall have to leave you alone at times and they may come when I am beyond call."

"As I obsarbed dat wouldn't make no diff'rence, 'cause dey doan' hab nuffin to do wid me. It mought be anoder thing if Mr. Hartley lit on me wid a cartwhip, but he'll neber come way up here fur me, 'cause he doan' know I'm here, — likewise Harv and his folks doan' know nuffin 'bout it neither. No matter where yo' stow me away Perfesser, I'll stay dere till yo' am ready to come fur me."

The man looked at Bunk with a prolonged, penetrating stare that chilled him through. Then in his cavernous voice he slowly said:

"When-you-disobey-me, you-will-die!"

"Yas, sir;" whispered the terrified youth.

The Professor stepped to the bench at his side, reached up and took a bottle of colorless liquid from a shelf. Withdrawing the glass stopper he handed it to the lad:

"Smell of that!" he commanded in the same awful tones.

Bunk's hand trembled so much that he came near dropping it.

"It won't blow me up?" he asked timidly.

"It won't hurt you! Do what you are told!"

The lad dared not hesitate. He held the compound to his nostrils and took several deep inhalations. It was a powerful soporific and in a minute or so he showed its effects. The Professor watched him, and at the proper moment took the bottle from his limp grasp.

"Now go back and sleep."

"Yas, sir," replied Bunk, who staggered to his couch, tumbled upon it and almost immediately sank into a heavy, dreamless slumber. It must have lasted a long time, for when he awoke the morning sun was shining through the open door. The Professor was not in the room, and after recalling his confused senses, Bunk rose from his bed. He was slightly dizzy from the effects of the drug and waited until he could steady himself before picking his way along the passage to the outside. He expected to see the aviator, but he was not in sight and a glance at the hangar showed it was empty. Professor Morgan and his helicopter were gone. Bunk was alarmed.

"I wonder if he's started for Afriky and furgot me! If he has he's played a low down trick."

Reflection removed this fear and he decided that his friend or enemy, as the case might be, had only gone to the village for his morning meal. Against that theory was the fact that he had taken his machine with him, or more properly the machine had taken him. With the distance so short, it was not reasonable that he would bother to make the trip by aerial sea.

Bunk sat down outdoors and tried to decide upon the best thing to do. Suddenly the thought came to him that it would not only help to pass away the dismal minutes of waiting, but would be the proper thing to write a letter to Mootsport. He entered the building again, stepping very gingerly, for he had a mortal terror of the wires and contraptions that were all around him. At the farther end of the room was a small desk, with paper, envelopes and pencils, but no ink. First peeping out of the door to make sure the Professor was not near, Bunk sat down on the bench provided and with pencil wrote a letter to Harvey. He paused with every labored word and listened. He knew he would detect the returning aviator in time to play the part of innocence. We remember the substance of that missive, which was the means of giving Harvey Hamilton his first tangible clue to the whereabouts of his colored friend.

The letter being finished, the problem of mailing it remained. It required a stamp and must be carried to the post office. Now there were fully a dozen stamps lying on a corner of the desk, but it was to Bunk's credit that he did not use one of them. Those little red rectangles were each worth two cents, while the value of the paper and envelope was so vague as to amount to nothing. It would be dishonest to appropriate a postage stamp, but not dishonest to use the other material. Bunk was always supplied with a moderate amount of funds and it occurred to him that it would be right to take a stamp provided he left a nickel in its place, thereby making generous payment for the accommodation.

"De Perfesser will notice it," was the belief that stayed his hand; "he told me not to send any letter home and if he finds out I've done it he'll blow me all to pieces."

He thrust the missive into his coat pocket and once more passed outside of the workshop. The location of the cabin as we know was in a lonely spot, and not a person was in sight. The village of Dawson lay within easy reach and he believed he could run thither and back before the return of the Professor. But he hesitated after passing down the path to where it met the highway. He felt that if seen by the aviator he could make the excuse that he was merely stretching his legs and had no thought of going farther.

While he stood debating whether to make a dash for it, good fortune favored him. Around a bend in the road, and approaching him, strode a man dressed as a farmer. He carried a rough staff in one hand and his trousers were tucked in the tops of his boots. He responded with a nod to Bunk's cheery "Good morning."

"Am yo' gwine to Dawson?" asked the African, though the course of the pedestrian made the question superfluous.

"That's what I've started to do, if I don't run off the track or bust my b'iler," was the characteristic reply.

"Will yo' please mail dis lub letter fur me?"

The man accepted the envelope and squinted at it.

"I don't see any stamp onto it."

Bunk handed him a quarter of a dollar.

"If yo' will put a stamp on it yo' may keep de change."

"All right, sonny, I'll act as mail carrier all day at them rates."

"And yo' mustn't say nuffin 'bout it to nobody."

The man promised and went on his way.

CHAPTER XX
A CHANGE OF QUARTERS

AFTER administering the drug which sent Bunk into dreamland Professor Morgan, having rested only a short time, resumed his work. He grudged the time he had already wasted as he viewed it, and toiled with absorbed earnestness until an exclamation of impatience showed he had run against a snag. In experimenting with a score of subtle fluids he discovered that one important ingredient was exhausted. He must obtain more before he could go on with his work. The chemical was quite common and he knew it was easy to obtain in Albany, which was not much more than a hundred miles distant as the crow or aeroplane flies. He could make the trip well within four hours and decided to do so. Since the leading drug stores kept open through the night there was no need of his delaying. He went to the hangar, ran out his helicopter and left without awaking Bunk, who he thought was likely to sleep all the time he was gone.

It was beginning to grow light when the strange machine was revealed by its flitting searchlight to many of the early risers in the capital of the State. As it gave out no noise, its appearance, absurdly exaggerated, was heralded throughout the country. Stories of a strange colossal airship which prowled through the heavens only in the night time had been published and some of the yellow journals had given illustrations of its appearance. This one was declared at first to be the same mysterious visitant of the upper regions, but the fact that the Dragon of the Skies made its descent in the heart of the city and that the single occupant stepped out and made a purchase at the most prominent drug store, robbed the account of its most thrilling feature.

Professor Morgan did not return at once. He snubbed those who gathered round with their numberless questions. Hiring two trustworthy men to guard his machine he went to an all-night restaurant and ate an early breakfast which he meant should serve until night, since it took too much time to lunch at noon. Then he decided to do still more in the way of economizing the minutes by buying supplies for Bunk, who had the faculty of being hungry morning, noon and night. The markets were open and he had no trouble in securing what he wanted. Biscuits, sugar, salt, pepper, meat, condensed milk; in fact, all that a rugged and growing lad could ask for were stowed in a large basket which was adjusted on the seat near the tank. They added considerable to the weight of the aeroplane, but much less than it was accustomed to carry in the person of Bohunkus Johnson.

The crowd that remained staring at the helicopter saw an amazing sight when a horizontal wheel directly beneath began revolving as the aviator took his seat, and the machine soared aloft smoothly, gracefully and in a line as truly vertical as if drawn by a mathematician. Nothing of the kind had ever been heard of before.

Bunk having despatched his letter through the kindness of the countryman, hurried back to the workshop and seated himself on the little bench in front to await the return of the Professor. He thus sat until the sun was well up in the sky, growing hungrier every minute and with his patience nearing its limit.

Removed from the presence of the terrible man he felt more free to indulge his meditations.

"I wonder if he thinks I'm gwine to sot here till I starve to death. He doan' keer 'bout eating hisself, but I ain't built dat way. I'll wait a little while longer and den if he doesn't come I'll go to de willage and eat eberyting in de old place. Golly! if dat ain't him now!"

He was right, for in the clear sky to the southward he saw the well-remembered Dragon of the Skies, with wings outspread, approaching at its usual swift pace. In less time than would be supposed, the aeronaut settled to rest and Bunk hurried forward to give the aid he could.

"Let me help yo' out, Perfesser," said he, extending his hand, but the other gave no heed. Turning, he lifted the big basket from the seat and placed it on the ground.

"Leave the car where it is," he commanded; "for we'll need it again in a few minutes."

"Yas, sir;" replied the lad, looking longingly at the willow receptacle.

"I have brought you enough food to last a week," said the Professor.

"Gee!" muttered Bunk, "it looks as if dere am jest 'nough for breakfast, but I'll worry 'long if you say so."

"Help yourself."

Bunk needed no second invitation. The man passed into the building, leaving him outside. He slid off the cover of the basket and his eyes sparkled at sight of the goodly stock of supplies. He did not pause in his feasting until one-half the contents had been placed where it would do the most good. He was drawing the back of his hand across his mouth when the Professor came out, bringing with him the blanket that had served Bunk while asleep.

"I'm going to take you to your new quarters," he explained. "My gracious!" he added, glancing at the wrecked food, "have you left anything?"

"I guess dere am 'nough for a bite," grinned Bunk.

"You're a wonder that I never saw equalled; let's be off."

The blanket and basket were carefully put in place, Bunk took his seat and the Professor after glancing over the machine to make sure that all was right assumed his usual position and set the uplifter spinning. So perfect was the working of the machine that there was no evidence of the increased weight it carried. Straight up in the air it rose for a hundred feet and then headed to the northward. As it approached the wild region to which we have referred several times the aviator slackened his pace as much as he could while retaining buoyancy, leaned out and scanned the ground over which he was sailing. It did not take him long to decide upon a landing place, and he descended at the spot which was visited by Dick Hamilton some days later.

Bunk had also made good use of his eyes. He noticed the cabin of guide Akers, the beautiful little lake beyond, the tent on the shore and the forms near it, to whom he waved his usual salutation, and closely studied the surroundings when they sank to the earth again.

As soon as the two felt the earth under their feet, they began a search which was quickly ended by the discovery of the cavern which has also been described.

"This will do," was the comment of the Professor after scanning it; "you couldn't ask for anything better."

Bunk surveyed the opening with mingled feelings. It certainly offered secure shelter against a storm, which was about all that could be said of it. Wishing to please his master he remarked:

"I allers sleeps wid my winder open at home and it'll be de same here and dis soots me. I wouldn't mind if I had some carpets or rugs and a peanner, but I can git along very well as it am."

"Carry in the basket," commanded the master, leading the way with the blanket over his arm. He flung it down at the rear of the cavern and Bunk set the receptacle beside it. Then the two walked outside, where they stood beside the aeroplane.

"Before I go," said the Professor in his most awesome tones, "I have a few things to say to you which you must not forget on your peril."

"Yas, sir."

"This is to be your home till I call to take you to Africa."

"Yas, sir."

"The time will go slowly to you, but here you must stay!"

"Yas, sir."

"When you grow tired of sleeping and eating you may walk through the woods, but take care that you don't go so far that you can't find your way back quickly and surely."

"Yas, sir."

"Confound you!" exclaimed the Professor suddenly, "can't you say anything but 'yas, sir'?"

"No, sir,-dat is-yas, sir," replied the confused Bunk, startled by the words and manner of the man.

"Well, then, why don't you say something else?"

"Yas, sir."

The Professor saw that it was useless to protest and therefore ignored the provoking response.

"I have important work awaiting me and must now return to my shop," he said in a gentler voice.

"When will yo' come back?"

"I intend to call each morning, unless something unexpected prevents."

"Yo' won't forgit to bring some wittles wid yo' each time, Perfesser?"

"I shall see that your wants in that respect are met; unless," he grimly added, "the supply in Dawson gives out."

"Yo' can reach oder towns if dat tooks place," suggested Bunk, with no suspicion of the sarcasm of the other remark.

"Bear in mind what I have said: this is to be your home until we are ready to start across the ocean."

"Yas, sir."

"If any strangers come near, you don't give them a word of explanation. Avoid having anything to do with them."

At that time, Professor Morgan had no knowledge that Harvey Hamilton was or rather soon would be on his track. He therefore made no reference to him, since he did not think it possible that he would become a factor in the problem. He stepped into his seat, and without saying anything further hied away to his workshop. He was impatient to resume his experimentation now that he had the lacking chemical.

At last Bohunkus Johnson found himself alone in the wilds of the southern Adirondacks. He did not need to be reminded that if he wished company he did not have to travel many miles to find it. He was within reach of settlements, and scattered houses and it was no difficult walk to that tent on the shore of the placid lake. But the African trip was an obsession with him. His heart was set on the voyage, of whose perils he never dreamed. Nothing could quench that longing except its realization or death itself.

"I'll do jest as de Perfesser says," he said to himself; "I'm sorry I sent dat letter home, for mebbe dere was someting in it which will set Harv onto my track,—but I can't think what it am onless—"

He almost dropped to the ground in dismay.

"I didn't put any name to de top of de page, but de postmaster has stamped de word 'Dawson' on de enwollop. Jee whizz! I neber thought ob dat!"

You will remember that it was this fact which told Harvey the one thing he needed to know in order to make an intelligent search for his friend. It was too late now to correct the error, and it was well for Bunk that he did not recall certain other words in his letter which gave invaluable aid to his friend. He found great relief in the belief that the start across the ocean would be made in a day or two at the furthest.

It must be admitted that Bunk's situation in more than one respect was trying. In the first place, he had no firearms, no such thing being thought necessary when he and Harvey Hamilton first left home with their biplane. He had not so much as a fishing line with which to beguile the hours that could not fail to become wearisome. He had been promised food and could not doubt that the Professor would see that he did not suffer for nourishment.

The first day spent in and about the cavern was tedious, though a goodly part of it was passed in eating and sleeping.

When darkness at last began closing in there was nothing left of the supplies that had been brought in the basket.

"If de Perfesser forgits me and doan' come in de morning," reflected Bunk, "I'll be in an orful fix, but I can always rampage frough de country. I've got 'nough money to buy a good deal and when dat runs out I can grab things 'permiscuous.'"

His idea of the wild animals that haunt the Adirondacks was vague. He knew that deer, bears, and he believed wolves were met with at times in different parts. Had he passed through Harvey's experience he might have become more disquieted. He suspected that tigers, leopards, lions, giraffes and possibly elephants were to be met with in the wilder portions, but the reliance upon which he always fell back was the conviction that none of these creatures knew how to climb a tree, while he was master of the art.

"I wish dis cave had a door dat I could shet, but it doan' hab nuffin ob de kind and if any ob dem critters walks into de front I'm catched for dere ain't any way out ob de back."

Investigation had told him that the one yawning opening was the only means of ingress and egress, because of which fact he studied a long time the problem of the safest thing to do. Suddenly it flashed upon him.

"I'll roost ebery night! Why didn't I thunk ob dat afore?"

Before darkness fully closed in, he left the cavern and began a careful tour of the immediate neighborhood. It did not require long to find a refuge that seemed to be specially prepared for him. It was a broad, branching oak, whose trunk was so huge that, to his disappointment, he saw no way of climbing it. His predicament was the reverse of the ursus species, for such a big shaggy stairs would have been easy for a bear to ascend. Slowly circling the forest monarch and using his strong eyes well in the obscurity, he soon fixed upon the means of making his way into the branches. It was, in short, to use a smaller tree which grew so close to the oak that their branches interlocked.

CHAPTER XXI
BUNK CAMPS OUT

BUNK'S expertness in climbing served him well. With no trouble he rapidly ascended the maple, whose trunk was six inches or more in diameter and whose branches with their soft, green foliage were interlocked with the more rugged limbs of the immense oak. The lowest branch of the latter was ten inches thick, and put out horizontally at a height of ten feet or more from the ground. It would have made a tree of itself.

When the youth found himself among the foliage he was able to discern in the fast increasing darkness the main limb. It was so near that, carefully balancing himself, he swung out and let go of his own support. The feat was not difficult and he seized the rugged support, which dipped considerably, but would have sustained a far greater weight without breaking. He crept over it to the massive trunk. It was in the crotch of this that he meant to make his couch for the night. He was too high to be in danger from any roving beasts, unless of the very largest kind.

"I 'spose an elephant might git me with his trunk, but I could hear him tramping the leaves and could scoot to the top of the tree. De worstest am a gerauf; they hab such long necks dat dey can pick de ball off a church steeple, but if I disremembers right dey doan' bite, but butt wid dere horns; dat lets me out."

Bunk had secured his perch, but the problem of making it a reposeful bed was a different matter. At first he tried sitting astride of the limb with his back against the trunk. This answered for a time, but soon became as onerous as the seat of Harvey Hamilton did when he was fleeing from the bear. Then he lay forward on his face along the limb, which he still bestrode. That was very little improvement and he had to give it up.

"De only way fur a feller to sleep am to lay down," he exclaimed disgustedly, "and dat's what I'm gwine to do."

He carefully extended his body along the shaggy support, face downward, steadying himself by grasping a smaller branch which put out from the larger. Having done this, Bunk held his place for a few minutes and then in trying to improve it rolled off the limb and dropped to the ground.

The distance was so trifling that he suffered no hurt though his feelings were much disturbed.

"I oughter fetched my blanket or laid some boards on de limbs; dat's what I'll do to-morrer if I can find de boards."

Nothing having been seen or heard to frighten him, he decided to go back to the cavern and spend his first night with only the partial protection he could find there. He had not as yet caught a glimpse of any wild animals and he did not believe he had cause to fear his own species. So he lay down and slept without waking until day came again.

At the brook which ran near, he bathed his face and hands, and then climbed to the most elevated portion of the rocks to await the Professor, who had promised to bring him breakfast. He was ravenously hungry, as was to be expected, and to his delight he was not forced to suffer long. The helicopter was really ahead of time and the aviator proved that he appreciated the appetite of the colored lad, who gave thanks for his thoughtfulness.

The man was alert and seemed to be in high spirits over the progress he had made. His manner was so noticeable that Bunk asked:

"How's yo' getting along, Perfesser?"

"Splendidly," was the reply; "everything is going right. I have completed my compound by which I can keep the machine going for two days; all that remains is to tune it up so as to be sure of making a hundred miles an hour. I shall do that to-day."

"Den we'll start for Afriky —"

"To-morrow. I must complete a few experiments first, but they are trifling and will result all right."

"Dat's good news," remarked the happy Bunk, catching the contagion; "yo'll find me ready as soon as yo' am."

"Have you seen anybody while I was away?"

"Nobody hain't been near here, but I can look down ober de lake and see folks afishing and de tent ober on t'other side."

"If any of them should wander up this way, don't let them see you. You will remember?"

"Yas, sir."

"I must be off, for every minute now counts."

"Yas, sir."

The Professor resumed his seat, set the uplifter spinning, slowly rose in the air until at the right elevation, when he darted southward like a swallow on the wing. Left to himself, Bunk began preparing for the tedious hours before him. He was eager to fit up a sleeping couch in the oak from which he had fallen the night before. He would have carried out his plan but for one drawback: he had no boards to serve him.

A bright idea struck him.

"I'll make a hammock; all I hab to do am to nail de corners on to de limbs and sleep jest like I do in my trundle bed at home."

The fact that not a nail was within reach did not deter him. Bringing the blanket from the cavern he slung it over one shoulder, climbed the sapling and readily picked his way among the branches of the oak. These were not placed as he wished, but after a good deal of work, no end of pains and considerable ingenuity, he managed to fasten the corners by twisting and tying them around the limbs until he had a fair imitation of the ordinary hammock with which we are all familiar. True, the center dipped lower than he wished, and when he gingerly trusted his weight to it the blanket sagged still more. In fact Bunk's position was much as if he were seated in the top of an open barrel with his head and feet protruding through the opening.

"Dere's one big adwantage ob dis," he reflected; "if de thing gibs way when I'm asleep I'll drap squar, so I'll be setting as if I'm in a chair when I hit de ground. Ef I gits tired I can flop ober; I'll try it."

With some difficulty he squirmed upon his face, with his heels almost touching the back of his head. The sensation was pleasant at first, but any unnatural position of the body is sure to become irksome in sleep, and it was to be feared that the lad would find his plan a failure when put to the test. He determined to try it, however, and came down to the ground satisfied with what he had accomplished.

"What the deuce are you trying to do?"

Bunk leaped off the ground and stared at the point whence the startling question had come. A middle-aged man, carrying a Winchester rifle, which rested in the hollow of his left arm, his smooth-shaven face expanded into a broad grin, had evidently been watching his actions for some minutes. The colored youth was so flustered that it must be said he did not do justice to himself in his replies.

"Why—why, I hung dat blanket up dere to dry."

"I don't see that it is wet."

"Wal, it will be when it rains and I wanter hab it ready."

"From the way you acted it looks as if you're trying to fix up a hammock among them limbs."

"Dats it!—dats it! I done forgot de name."

"Who are you?" demanded the man, looking sharply at him.

"Bohunkus Johnson, sah."

"A blamed queer name; what brought you here?"

Bunk was on the point of telling the truth, when he reflected that it might reveal more than Professor Morgan wished.

"I'm hunting deers," said he.

"Have you killed any?"

"Sartinly; I've killed 'leben."

"Where are they?"

"Laying round in de woods; haben't yo' seed any ob 'em?"

"Where's your gun?"

The man was firing his questions so fast that the bewildered Bunk floundered into deep water before he could check himself.

"I frowed it away."

"Why did you do that?"

"I had a fout wid de last buck and broke de lock ober his head; yo' see it warn't no use, so I frowed it ober de rocks."

"Sure you killed eleven deer?"

"Mought hab been two or free more, but dere war dat many sartin."

"Well, I'm a game warden and will take you along with me; I'm looking for just such scamps as you."

Bunk's jaw dropped and his knees shook.

"What—what yo' gwine to do wid me?"

"It's a thousand dollars fine for shooting a deer out of the season; twenty years in prison for killing two, and hanging by the heels till you're dead for scalping eleven."

The terrified Bunk collapsed. What a forceful illustration of the wisdom of telling the truth at all times! He had long been known at home as one who hated a falsehood, and now when he strayed momentarily from the right path the penalty was awful. He broke into a cackling laugh and in a tremulous voice said:

"I war joking, mister; I hain't killed no deers."

"I never thought you had; the next time you try to spin an outlandish yarn don't make quite so big a fool of yourself."

With which Jim Haley, who later met Dick Hamilton, turned on his heel and walked away.

Bunk scratched his head.

"Blamed if I doan' begin to think Deacon Buggs am right; he allers said at prayer meeting dat dere ain't no sense in sticking to a lie when yo're cotched in it. Dat feller talked so fast dat I couldn't git time to fix up my story. Next time I'll straighten out tings better."

With so many hours at command, the youth did more wandering through the surrounding solitude than before. He took particular care not to meet any persons because of a well founded fear that he could not withstand the fire of questions that would be leveled at him. Professor Morgan had assured him that the grand start would be made on the morrow, and Bunk must use every precaution against doing the least thing that would interfere with the plan. It was this dread which caused him suddenly to turn off when he found he was approaching the smoke of a camp fire which some party had kindled among the trees. He stole away until assured he was beyond danger of being seen by any of the strangers, whose friendship or lack of enmity toward him he could not doubt.

After a time Bunk turned his steps toward the lake, still resolute of purpose to keep clear of all persons, but he yielded to his curiosity regarding a canoe which was anchored near the northern end and not far from shore. In it were seated three men engaged in fishing. In the stillness he could hear them when they spoke, though he did not catch the words uttered. The trees, undergrowth and rocks gave him all the screen he could need in approaching the little party. When he had gone as far as was prudent, he stopped, still carefully concealing himself.

Suddenly one of them laughed. Something familiar in the sound startled the lad, who, shading his eyes with one hand, peered intently at the group. A moment later he gasped:

"Gee! dat am Dick Hamilton!"

Then he recalled what he had heard before leaving home about Harvey's brother being on a vacation in the Adirondacks. Without suspecting it, Bunk had been brought to the neighborhood of his camp, which must be at the tent he had several times noticed. With this recollection the shiver of fear quickly passed. His first thought was that Dick had come thither to take him home and that one of his companions was Harvey. A scrutiny, however, showed that the other two were strangers.

Then he was comforted by the reflection that it was impossible for Harvey to know where he was.

This discovery convinced Bunk that he was running too great risk in venturing so close to the lake. If Dick Hamilton should see him he would call him to account and take measures to head off that trip to Africa. Accordingly, he stealthily withdrew and when beyond all danger of being observed he hurried to his quarters up the mountainous slope.

The question he asked himself was whether he should tell Professor Morgan what he had learned. He decided there was no need to do so. From his elevated station he kept an eye upon the canoe in the lake. He saw at the end of two or more hours that the party were through fishing for the time. One of them began swinging the paddle, and the canoe glided southward and turned into the small inlet at the back of the camp, where it was drawn up the shingle and the trio walked to the tent. Although the distance did not prevent Bunk from seeing the figures, and he was sure he could distinguish Dick Hamilton, he was unable to note their features, and but for the close view he had obtained he would not have suspected the identity of his friend.

"Dick am more rambunctious dan Harv," reflected Bunk, "and it won't do fur him to know I'm in dis part ob de world. When I come back from Afriky I'll tell him de whole story and he'll laugh as much as me."

CHAPTER XXII
FACE TO FACE AT LAST

SO far as sleeping in a hammock suspended a dozen feet above ground was concerned, Bunk's attempt was as much a failure as his effort to rest among the limbs of the oak on the previous night. In disgust he gave it up, and yanking the blanket free went back to the cavern and again slept without disturbance. The weather continued so mild that the covering gave him all the protection he needed.

When Professor Morgan made his appearance in the morning, not quite as early as before, Bunk saw he was not in such buoyant spirits as on his last call. Something had gone wrong. He made no replies to the lad's questions, but when about to leave him for the day, explained:

"Things haven't come out as I anticipated; I shall have to go to Albany again to get a new chemical; the last was not pure; do you understand?"

"Yas, sir."

"You don't understand a word I said to you," snorted the man; "why do you pretend you do?"

"Yas, sir."

With an angry grunt the aviator mounted his seat, started the uplifter revolving and sailed away without another word.

Several days now passed so similar in all respects that it is not worth while to dwell upon them. The Professor remained glum and sour and Bunk held him in too great awe to repeat any questions after his first curt snubbing. He made his sleeping quarters in the cavern, ate and wandered through the neighborhood, watching people at a distance and always keeping out of their sight. Had he possessed a field glass like Harvey Hamilton, he would have made some discoveries that would have interested and alarmed him.

We come now to the day of the disastrous search made by the Hamilton brothers. Bunk was sitting at the mouth of the cavern and beginning to feel drowsy when his nerves were set tingling by the whistled signal of the young man, who had almost come upon him. Had Dick refrained from giving that warning he would have been face to face with Bunk within the following five minutes.

"Dat's him!" gasped the negro, scooting behind the cavern and among the undergrowth, where he crouched low.

He not only heard every signal, but caught a glimpse of the young man. Had it been Harvey whom he saw he probably would have gone forward in response to the calls, but he dared not let the elder brother see him.

"I'd doot," muttered Bunk, whose conscience reproved him, "if I could be sure he wouldn't butt in and make trouble."

One fact lifted the spirits of Bunk to the highest notch. That morning Professor Morgan exultingly told him that he had attained complete success at last. The new chemical had done its work perfectly; the last obstacle had been overcome, and the start for distant Africa would be made the next day without fail. It was this announcement which caused the youth to guard against discovery by his friend. Of course he did not dream that Harvey Hamilton was in the vicinity.

Bunk was in such a fluster over the knowledge that his dismal days in this mountain retreat were ended that he slept little. This was his last night in the cave and the wonderful voyage was to begin on the morrow.

Upon what trivial incidents do the most important events often turn! Professor Morgan told the truth when he asserted that he had reached the end of his experimentation. He had solved the magical combination of chemical agents by which the supply of fuel for his helicopter would serve for more than two days without renewal. Having done this, all that remained was to finish his preparations for leaving the continent and voyaging over the Atlantic. His machine worked so superbly that he had no fear of any storm he might encounter, though he wisely decided to study weather probabilities before making his venture. Repeated tests convinced him that an average speed of eighty miles was easy to maintain. This would require a trifle less than thirty-three hours to go from Quebec to Liverpool, his intention from the first being to start from the former city.

The change he made in his programme was this: instead of leaving Quebec, he would make his starting point on the New Jersey coast, not far below Sandy Hook, with his destination the island of St. Vincent, of the Cape Verde group, off the coast of Africa. This route is three hundred miles longer than the other, but as he viewed it the fact was not worth considering because of the new fuel he had invented. It was not far from St. Vincent to the African coast, and he preferred not to land in England because of the excitement his feat would cause.

So long as his purpose was to depart from Quebec, he intended to lay in the necessary stock of provisions in that city, deferring the work until the last moment. But this was sure to bring unpleasant notoriety, and he now saw an easy escape from it. No large amount of supplies would be needed and he could procure them at the Washington Hotel in Dawson. As for himself, he did not mind fasting for a couple of days, but he knew how it was with his assistant. He therefore proceeded to stock up in the little country town, because of which his usual morning call upon Bohunkus Johnson was delayed, and it was that same delay which gave the necessary time for the happening of more than one important event.

Had Bunk not been impatient over the tardiness in the return of Professor Morgan, he would have paid attention to the two persons in the canoe at the end of the lake. He would have seen them leave the craft and disappear among the trees and undergrowth that lined the sheet of water, but he noted nothing of the kind. It is doubtful which emotion was the stronger within him,—the desire for satisfying his craving for food, or his eagerness to start upon the aerial voyage to the Dark Continent. He took his station in front of the cavern and scanned the heavens to the south, wondering what could keep the aviator away so long.

"He oughter hurry up, 'cause it am a long way and we've waited so many days dat dere ain't no sense ob waiting longer."

Hark! What was that which fell upon his ear? It sounded like the whistle which he had heard so many times when he and Harvey or Dick Hamilton were calling to each other.

"Can't be Harv," he whispered, "'cause he am ten thousand miles away; must be dat Dick is poking round here agin."

This time there was no mistake. The signal was so clear and sharp that Bunk turned sharply and stared at the point whence it came. He was struck speechless when he saw the smiling Harvey walk toward him.

"Hello, Bunk! I'm glad to see you."

For one moment the lad stood transfixed, and then overwhelmed by the threatened calamity, as it seemed to him, he wheeled and made a dash for the other side of the open space, where was the pile of rocks that had served him as headquarters for a number of days. He had almost reached them when to his consternation Dick Hamilton stepped forth and confronted him. Escape was shut off.

"Well, my blooming idiot, what have you to say for yourself? I have a great mind to kick you all the way from here to Mootsport. This is a pretty chase you have given us; you aren't worth half the trouble you have caused."

Bunk gaped, but did not attempt reply. Suddenly he turned to run in the opposite direction, but Harvey had drawn nigh and was within arm's reach.

"Try it if you want to," said Dick, pretending to raise his Winchester; "I should like to prove how quick I can drop you."

For the first time the lad found his tongue, though both listeners noted the quaver in his voice:

"What yo' want to shoot me fur, Dick? I hain't done nuffin to yo'."

Harvey was softer hearted than his brother.

"We are not going to hurt you, Bunk, but you deserve to have the worst trouncing you ever received in your life. It seems to me you have been a long time getting started for Africa."

"I'm expecting de Perfesser, Harv, ebery minute; dis am de morning dat we am to go."

"Well," said Dick, as he came still nearer, "that little trip is indefinitely postponed."

This declaration roused Bunk. He knew the brothers would interfere with him if they gained the chance, and now they were doing so, for of a surety the two were in accord.

"See yere, Dick, yo' hain't got nuffin to do wid dis; you ain't my boss."

"Do you want me to prove that I am; here, Harv, hold my gun for a minute while I show Bunk that I'm his boss."

The words of revolt had roused the temper of the younger, who accepted the weapon from Dick's hand, quite content that he should chastise the ungrateful lad.

But the dusky youth had no liking for a struggle of that nature. It would have been fun for the young athlete, figuratively speaking, to wipe the ground with him. Dick had demonstrated his ability in that direction more than once. He doubled his fists and stepped in front of Bunk.

"Put up your hands and we'll settle the question in the next three minutes."

"I doan' want nuffin to do wid yo'," growled the negro, edging to one side; "but I'd like to know if I hain't de right to do as I blamed please."

"No; for you haven't the sense of a one-eyed owl with the pip. Why didn't you ask permission of Mr. Hartley to go on this tomfool trip?"

"I didn't hab de chance."

"When you wrote that letter to Harv and told him you were in this part of the country, you could have asked Mr. Hartley's consent."

"What's dat?" demanded Bunk; "I didn't tell yo' nuffin; what yo' talkin' 'bout?"

Harvey interposed just then and showed the thick-witted lad how his second letter gave the clue they needed, as proof of which the young man was here on the ground, with his aeroplane but a few miles away. When the absurd truth penetrated Bunk's head his self-disgust was amusing.

"Gee! I neber thunk ob dat; warn't I a big fool?"

"You have never been anything else," replied Dick; "when you get back home I shall advise Mr. Hartley to tie a rope round your leg and fasten the other end to a fence post; you are not fit to be trusted alone."

Bunk did not resent these disrespectful allusions, but it galled him sorely to see his life ambition snatched from him.

"I doan' see why yo' try to stop me."

"We're not trying, Bohunkus,—we're doing it," replied Dick with a meaning grin; "if you have any doubt remaining I shall be glad to remove it."

Bunk was in a torturing dilemma. He saw the one enrapturing dream of his life, just on the verge of fulfillment, about to be dissipated like a wreath of vapor. If Professor Morgan had kept his promise and come to this meeting place at the usual hour, they would now be on their way to the "land of hope." And, as we know, he would have arrived on time but for his change of plan which led him to stock up at the little hotel in Dawson instead of doing so at another stage of the trip.

On the other hand a lion stood in the path in the person of Dick Hamilton, who left no doubt of his purpose of checking the mad scheme before the first real step could be taken. Bunk was well enough acquainted with the young man to know he was in earnest and would carry out every threat he had made. The lad began to wheedle. In a whimpering voice he asked:

"What's de use ob treating me dis way?"

"What way?" demanded the implacable Dick.

"Stopping my going to Afriky; I neber done nuffin to yo', so why do yo' use me so blamed mean?"

Dick was fast losing patience, but Harvey felt sympathy for the misguided lad.

"Bunk, do you know that Professor Morgan is crazy?" he asked.

The negro started as if stung.

"Yo' doan' mean dat, Harv!"

"I surely do; he is as crazy as a June bug and has been for a long time."

Plainly Bunk was impressed. He stared at his friend and then administered a sharp reproof by asking:

"Why didn't yo' tell me dat afore?"

"I ought to have done so, and am sorry I didn't."

"If you hadn't been the champion idiot you would have found it out in five minutes for yourself."

It was Dick who said this.

"I knowed he acted mighty qu'ar sometimes and said cur'ous tings dat I didn't understand, but I neber thought he was out of his head."

"Sometimes he has as much sense as you —"

"Umph! if he doesn't have a hundred times as much," interrupted Dick, "he's not only crazy but the biggest fool in Christendom. Now I suppose you are ready to turn your back on him and go home with us."

"Dunno 'bout dat."

"Well, here comes the Professor, Dick, and you must settle with him," said Harvey.

CHAPTER XXIII
MILO MORGAN'S WATERLOO

THE three caught sight of the helicopter in the same instant. The strange machine was rushing through the air like a colossal eagle. Professor Morgan had seen the group while some distance away and headed for it, sailing at a height of less than two hundred feet and rapidly descending. Instead of approaching in a direct line, he made a sweeping circle and came down in the ordinary way by volplaning instead of making use of his uplifter.

While these manœuvres were going on Dick Hamilton stepped across to his brother and reached out his hand.

"Let me have the rifle, Harv; it looks as if we're going to have lively times."

"Gee!" gasped the terrified Bunk; "yo' ain't gwine to shoot him!"

"That depends; if you try any tantrums I may have to plug you first. Understand, Bunk, that you are to stand back and not open your mouth or do a thing till I give you permission."

"Yas, sir."

Harvey would have made protest, for he was filled with shuddering dread, but he realized that for the present he stood in the same situation as Bunk. The big brother had stepped to the front and taken charge of affairs. Moreover, he never forgot the truth that in dealing with an insane person you must first impress him with the fact that you do not hold him in the slightest fear. While as a rule it is not wise to dispute or argue or try to turn him aside from his purpose by force, occasions may arise like the present when no other course is possible.

Professor Morgan must have read the meaning of the sight that brought him to the spot. He recognized Harvey before he stepped out of his machine and his rage flamed up against him. Ignoring the other two, he strode toward the young aviator with clenched fists and with murder in his blazing eyes. In a thunderous bass he demanded:

"What business have you here? I'll teach you —"

He had said this much and his long legs were still in motion, when Dick leaped between them and holding his rifle at his hip with muzzle leveled at the infuriated man, he commanded:

"Stop! if you touch him I'll let daylight through you!"

The Professor halted and turned upon the other, his frame trembling with surcharged fury.

"I'll kill you!"

It is impossible to picture the frightful scene at this moment. Bunk Johnson was silent and awed. Harvey was a little to one side and in front of him, while in the other direction stood Dick, one foot advanced as if ready to bound forward, his right hand inclosing the lock of his gun, so that the forefinger could be seen crooked around the trigger. The weapon was so pointed that only a slight pressure was needed to send a bullet through the long gaunt body hardly a dozen feet away.

"All right," calmly replied Dick; "you can begin as soon as you please, my distinguished friend, but before you reach me you will have to stop ten spheres of lead and by that time I calculate

I shall be able to handle you without the need of my Winchester."

Professor Morgan may have been "off his base," but he could not fail to read the meaning of those words, backed up by the pose of him who uttered them. He stopped like a tiger baffled of his prey.

"Why don't you shoot?" he hissed.

"You haven't given me the excuse I'm waiting for; in the case of every one of the seven men I have shot my explanation secured my acquittal in the courts. I'm taking the same course with you."

The sight of Harvey seemed to concentrate once more the lunatic's resentment against him. But for the presence of that Winchester and the man behind the gun, he would have rended the youth, provided the latter did not stand him off with his Colt.

"What business, I demand, have you to come here?"

"Please address your remarks to me," said Dick; "I'm boss of this job and that brother of mine over there hasn't a word to say. He came up here, I may tell you, to take Bohunkus Johnson home with him, and he's going to do it as sure as two and two make four. If you have any views to express on the situation do so now or forever after hold your peace."

Checked thus the Professor turned toward the paralyzed Bunk.

"Do you wish to go with me to Africa?"

"Yas, sir."

"Have these people any right to stop you?"

"Yas, sir."

"Oh!" exclaimed the Professor, with the first oath that his two listeners had ever heard him utter, "have done with that damnable 'Yas, sir!' I'm tired of hearing it."

"Yas, sir," replied Bunk, who must not be blamed, for really he hardly knew whether he was standing on his head or feet.

"I have brought food to last our trip and everything is ready. Go to your seat in the machine and we will start at once."

"Yas, sir," responded the negro lad, taking a step in the direction of the monoplane, only to find that Dick Hamilton was as alert as before.

"Back with you! If you want to save what little brains you have don't take another step in that direction."

Poor Bunk halted and stared in wretched perplexity at the young man. Could Professor Morgan at that moment have caught his eye, he would have controlled him absolutely through that mysterious hypnotic power with which nature had endowed him. But it was Dick who now held him enchained.

"Bunk, start for the lake and start a-running. When you get there, wait for us. GO!"

The lad broke into a headlong dash, shouting at the top of his voice:

"Murder! fire! robbers! thieves! sabe me!"

And he kept it up until he crashed out of sight of the three who remained behind. By a tremendous effort, Dick Hamilton maintained his sternness of expression. As for Harvey, he did not try to restrain his silent laughter. It was the most comical incident he had seen in many a day. Professor Morgan glared and was mute. He seemed utterly at a loss and unable to grasp the situation.

"My dear Professor," said Dick addressing him, "don't you think it is about time you ended this call? We are growing a little weary of you."

"Are you my master?" asked the lunatic in his sepulchral voice.

"It looks that way just now; if you have any doubt let's test it."

Harvey wished to ask one or two questions, but thought it would be unwise. It was clear that the Professor hated him unspeakably for the overthrow of his plans. No doubt, as has been said, he would have leaped upon the youth but for that other young man who held a deadly Winchester in his grasp. It should not be thought that Harvey felt any personal fear. He had his revolver at command and would have used it if necessary to save his own life, but he dreaded any such an issue unspeakably.

"Professor," said Dick in the even tone he had used from the first, "why don't you start for Africa? You won't have Bunk for a companion and you are gaining nothing by this delay. How long do you think you will be on the road?"

Harvey could not prevent himself from saying:

"I hope the Professor won't try it."

"It's easy to prevent him, if you wish it."

"How?"

"Which is the most vulnerable part of his helicopter?"

"I am not sure; why?"

"It strikes me that the tank will answer best for a target; I can put a bullet through that and let out all that wonderful fluid which is to furnish his motive power. I rather think the Professor will have to make a little longer delay, and in the meantime we can see that he is placed in an asylum, where he belongs."

"What's the use of this dilly-dallying?" suddenly broke out Dick Hamilton, whose patience was ended. "Professor, if you don't board that machine and go back to your workshop at Purvis, I'll bore a hole through it and then perforate you similarly. Step lively! Get a move on you!"

"I'm not through with you!" warned the aviator, still quivering with rage; "I go, but I return and will make you rue this hour!"

"By-by; I shall be ready for you whether you call by day or at night."

With two bounds the lunatic reached his machine, sprang into his seat, jerked the lever which controlled the uplifter, and began rising from the earth. As soon as he was clear of his surroundings, he sailed away at terrific speed, and it was noticeable that he headed south, which was in the direction of his Purvis workshop.

CHAPTER XXIV
A NEW RISK

"WOULD I have shot Professor Morgan?" repeated Dick Hamilton in recalling the incidents just related to his friends in camp. "Not for the world. I should no more have fired at that poor fellow than I should have slain—well, say that buck with the big antlers."

"But you made frightful threats against him."

"All pure bluff; I didn't mean a word of it; you know that the first step to secure mastery of a lunatic is to make him afraid of you. I found it rather hard work in the Professor's case, but think I succeeded."

"What would you have done if he had attacked me, as he started to do?" asked Harvey.

"I knew you had your Colt and that each chamber was loaded, but before you could have drawn and fired, I should have thrown away my rifle and leaped upon him. His build and looks show he is a lithe, wiry fellow, but I should have mastered him. It might have been a hard struggle and some ugly blows would have been struck and they would have been a cause of keen regret, for you can't feel enmity against an irresponsible person. But by keeping up the bluff I headed him off."

This brief extract from the conversation of the group at the tent by the lake was closed by the following curious remark of the elder Hamilton:

"If it hadn't all turned out as it did, I never should have appreciated the wit and brightness of this handsome brother of mine. What he did afterward was as much ahead of my performance as the United States of America is ahead of every other nation in the world."

Which remark compels us to return to the scene of the meeting near the cavern where Bohunkus Johnson was waiting for the Professor to take him on his aerial voyage to Africa.

Harvey was still laughing over the frenzied flight of the colored youth when he suddenly sobered at the fear that the inventor would follow with his machine and pick up Bunk before he could be prevented; but the crazy aviator did not seem to have such a thought, for, as has been said, he sailed straight for his workshop.

There was no reason for the brothers remaining and they started after the lad, who was found by the canoe still bewildered and scared almost out of his wits.

"Whar's—whar's de Perfesser?" he asked in a tremulous voice.

"Didn't you see him going back to his shop in his monoplane?"

"I seed de machine but I didn't know he war in it."

"Suppose he had come here for you?" inquired Dick.

"He wouldn't hab got me."

"How would you have escaped him?"

"I'd crawled under de canoe and stuck my nose up on toder side where he couldn't see me, and breeved so soft he'd thought I was drownded."

"That idea is as brilliant as most of the others you have formed."

"Gee! if I'd knowed he was crazy I'd knocked his head off and den run like blazes for hum," said Bunk, anxious to placate his friends whom he had so grievously offended. They understood his feelings and did not press him. Dick motioned for the lad to take his place in the boat and the two followed, the elder picking up the paddle and heading for the tent where Val Hunter and Fred Wadsworth were awaiting them with much curiosity.

"We saw the monoplane," said the Southerner, "and wondered what was going on. So this is Bunk, is it?" he added, gravely extending his hand to the abashed youth, who mumbled something unintelligible. He was made welcome and the brothers withheld all criticism in his presence. Dick went so far as to remark that if Bunk had had any suspicion of the lunacy of the man, events would have turned out very differently. This delighted the fellow, who began to appreciate the invaluable kindness that had been done him by Dick and Harvey.

He was eager to show his good will toward all by doing the chores in camp. There was always more or less work of that nature, such as gathering wood for the oven or furnace or whatever it might be called, the dressing and cooking of fish, and the preparation of other articles for dinner. While the lad was busy with these duties, the four young men gathered in front of the tent, most of them smoking, and held a conversation that was destined to have important results.

"Why did the Professor resent so fiercely your keeping Bunk from him?" asked Wadsworth, "he couldn't have placed much value on so slow-witted a lad."

"It was one of the idiosyncrasies of a disordered brain. Had he been perfectly sane he would have cared little about him," replied Dick.

"I have been thinking," remarked Hunter, "that something ought to be done to prevent that poor genius from committing suicide."

"I think the same," added Harvey.

"You feel sure he intends to try to cross the Atlantic?"

"He is certain to make the venture unless prevented."

"How can you hold a madman in check?" asked Dick; "I almost regret that I didn't send a bullet through the tank of his machine."

"It wouldn't have taken him long to repair the fracture," said Hunter.

"It would have delayed him several days, and in the meantime we could lay the case before the authorities and ask them to interfere."

"I doubt it," replied Hunter thoughtfully; "I can't see on what ground the law could prevent him from going on with his experiments. Suppose he proved — what I believe is true — that the chemical combination which he has made will buoy his aeroplane two days or more and that he can travel a hundred miles an hour, what right would any one have to interfere with him? No; there must be other plans tried, or we shall have to leave him to his fate."

"What do you mean by other plans?" asked Harvey.

"I'll be hanged if I know; can't you think of something?"

Harvey made an evasive answer; for in truth, he was turning over a scheme in his mind which he was afraid to make known. Dick, taking advantage of his commanding position as an older brother, would likely put a veto upon it. Besides, Harvey was not yet certain he would try it even with their assent.

"Dick," he said, "you mustn't forget one thing."

"What is that?"

"The threat made by the Professor; he warned you that he was not through with you."

"Another vaporing of a disordered brain," replied Dick airily.

"None the less it must not be forgotten," added Hunter; "I know of the case of a lunatic in Mississippi who was offended by an old friend, and who nursed his revenge for more than three years and then assassinated his unsuspecting comrade of former days."

"What can the Professor do to hurt us?"

Harvey recalled the incident of the Professor blowing up the kidnappers' cabin in eastern Pennsylvania.

"He manufactures and carries at times torpedoes of the most destructive nature. Suppose he circles above us and drops a half dozen on our heads or this tent."

"In that case," said Dick, "we should be justified in using our rifles and I calculate we could do it before he got in his work."

"He may wait till we are all asleep inside."

"Which makes me regret the more that I didn't put his machine out of commission when I had the chance."

"I don't see that that would have done much good," said Harvey, "for he could steal up to the tent in the dark on foot."

"Or might wait until the aeroplane was repaired and he had gotten a new supply of fuel," suggested Wadsworth.

"The only hope, as it strikes me," observed Hunter, "is that in his anxiety to be off on his trip he won't delay to even up things with you folks. But, as I told you, my knowledge of lunatics points the other way."

"It looks as if we shall have a call from our distinguished friend," said Wadsworth, who, however did not seem to be much disturbed over the prospect.

"What do you advise?" asked Dick.

"There are two or three things we might do. Suppose we hang round here this afternoon, taking turns in playing chess, and not forgetting to keep a lookout for squalls. If the gentleman comes booming down this way, we can draw ourselves up in line and receive him with a proper military salute. We have Colts and a Winchester repeater, and if we all let fly together one or two of the bullets ought to find the bull's eye, and we can blaze away before he is near enough to drop any of his pills of dynamite."

Although none noticed the fact, Harvey Hamilton took no further part in the conversation. He was pondering over the scheme that came into his mind some time before.

"He is too cunning to offer such an opening; I gave him so good a scare with my little gun that he doesn't want to run against it."

"What do you think he will do?" asked Wadsworth.

"I haven't much fear of him; he was so cowed that he is likely to give me a wide berth."

"There's where you make a mistake," said Hunter; "we are not through with him yet; if we do not receive a call from him between now and to-morrow morning, I shall miss my guess."

At this point in the conversation Harvey Hamilton rose to his feet and yawned.

"If you don't mind, I'll leave you for awhile."

"Where are you going?" asked his brother.

"I shall walk to the home of Aunt Hep and call upon her and Miss Harbor."

"Hadn't you better tarry till after our dinner?"

"I shall be in time to get a meal there that's worth eating," replied Harvey with a smile; "you needn't wait for me."

"I don't think we shall after that," replied his brother; "if you aren't more courteous you won't get any supper."

"Aunt Hep will be charmed to have me stay there," remarked Harvey, who sauntered off, with never a thought on the part of the three that he was hiding his real purpose in thus leaving them for an indefinite time.

So afraid was Harvey that his errand would be suspected that he loitered until well beyond sight of his friends, when he hurried his pace. He arrived before the women had dinner ready and it need hardly be said they were glad to see him. In their brief acquaintance, and especially because of their memorable ride in the biplane, he had won his way to their regard.

"I'm going home to-morrow," said Ann Harbor.

"Why not wait a bit longer?" asked Harvey.

"That's what I've been trying to coax her to do," said her relative, "but when she takes it into her head to leave there's no holding her."

"I told paw I should not be gone long and he'll be real mad if I don't git back pretty soon."

"How would you like to have me take you in my airship?"

The girl's eyes sparkled.

"Oh that would be splendid; will you do it?"

"I think I may safely promise that I can give you the ride possibly to-morrow, and if not then by the next day at the latest."

"I'll wait," she said, aquiver with delight; "I was pretty well scared when we had our ride, but you managed everything so well that I ain't frightened the least bit."

"Why should you be? Maybe Aunt Hep will go with us."

"La sakes; I've been thanking the Lord ever since that my neck wasn't broke and I'll never tempt Providence that way again. You will spend the rest of the day with us?"

"No," replied Dick; "I can't even wait for dinner, though if I get back in time I shall be glad to have a meal with you."

CHAPTER XXV
"I'LL DO IT!"

HARVEY HAMILTON walked out to where his aeroplane was waiting, and under the eyes of Ann Harbor and her aunt set the propeller revolving, mounted his seat, called a cheery good-bye and sped away in the direction of Dawson. He had become so familiar with the section that there was no uncertainty in his course. He was not heading for the town, but veered slightly to one side, and when he caught sight of the workshop of Professor Milo Morgan, he aimed as straight for it as an arrow driven from a bow.

He was yet some distance off when he observed the man in front of his building, bending over his helicopter as if attending to some repair of the machinery. When the noise of the approaching biplane fell upon his ear, he straightened up, turned around and stared in amazement. He stood as rigid as a statue, never once removing his gaze from the biplane, which lightly touched the ground, scooted a few rods and came to a standstill less than fifty feet from where he was scrutinizing it, and the young aviator.

Harvey knew the critical moment had come. While stepping to the ground, he drew his revolver from his hip pocket, examined it for a moment and then shoved it back in place. This was a little by-play meant to warn the Professor that his visitor owned a deadly weapon and held it at instant command. It is to be noted that the man carried nothing of the kind. His skill as a chemist gave him more frightful agents, though he could not have called them into play, as the circumstances stood, before the youth would anticipate him.

Harvey faced him with a smile and walked forward.

"Good morning, Professor; may I have a little talk with you?"

"Have you come to shoot me?" asked the man, with a terrible glare. He could not forget his recent experience at the cavern, when he must have believed he stood on the very edge of death.

"That depends upon yourself," was the reply in the same pleasant voice; "I call upon you as a friend, but if you wish me to be an enemy I am prepared."

"What do you want?"

Throughout the remarkable interview which followed, neither sat down, and Harvey held his place a dozen paces away. This was prudent, for it was uncertain what the crank might attempt. So long as he was held off he could do no harm, for Harvey would forestall his slightest movement. The venomous hatred shown by him toward the youth because of his interference warned the latter to be on the alert, especially during the opening moments of their talk.

"I have a few words to say to you, Professor; are you willing to listen?"

"Say what you please, but if you had a grain of sense you would know better than to place yourself in my power."

"I haven't placed myself in your power and don't intend to do so; don't forget that. I wish to speak about your trip across the Atlantic."

"Well?"

"It is too bad that Bohunkus was prevented from going with you, but you will admit that he has no right to leave home without the permission of Mr. Hartley, with whom he lives."

"What has he got to do with it?" demanded the Professor, in a voice that sounded like the growl of a tiger.

"He is the master of Bohunkus; if you will get his consent, the colored lad will accompany you to Africa; nobody else will object."

"Then why did you and that fellow with you hold him back?" asked the Professor with an ominous gleam of his burning eyes.

"I have just told you the reason; we ought to have explained and I am sorry we forgot to do so. If you will sail down to Mootsport, see Mr. Hartley and persuade him to say yes, there will be no more trouble."

"I shan't do any such thing; I don't care about the boy, only it made me mad to have you and the other scoundrel try to prevent my doing as I pleased."

"We were rough,—I'll admit it, and I beg to apologize."

Harvey was striving his hardest to win the good-will of the lunatic. Having impressed him with the fact that he did not hold him in fear, the young aviator was striving to placate and soothe him.

"Now," continued the caller, "every one must admit that you have made one or two of the most wonderful inventions of the century. Are you sure you can sail across the Atlantic with your machine?"

"Humph!" snorted the Professor, "you know I can; why do you ask such a question?"

"Suppose when you are well out over the ocean you run into a tempest or hurricane?"

"It will take me less than two days to cross and I can read the weather for that long; I know better than to run such a risk."

"Good! but you know the weather probabilities sent out by the government are not reliable far out at sea."

"I'm not depending on the government; I shall read the signs myself."

"Good again! But suppose some part of your machinery breaks down."

"It won't break down; it is made too well and has been tested too often."

"Or that that new kind of petrol or fluid should run short, owing to unexpected delays?"

"It won't run short; I shall take enough to carry me to the other side and half way back without renewal. You talk like an idiot."

"It is hard, Professor, to grasp your ideas, which stamp you as the equal of Edison in some respects. But may I offer a suggestion?"

This was said with so much deference that the inventor would have had to be a much more pronounced crank not to have been pleased. He growled:

"I'm listening; sometimes a fool can say something that a wise man should heed."

"I think you have hit it. What I wish to suggest is that before you start eastward you give your machine a decisive test."

"I have done so."

"But only for short distances; you have traveled two or three hundred miles and stayed in the air for ten or twelve hours. You know you must do a good deal better than that in order to reach the other side of the Atlantic."

"Don't you suppose I know all that and am prepared for it?"

"You will pardon me, Professor, but after you left us this morning I thought a good deal about you and your purpose. I became worried and could not help feeling that you were running too much risk when you headed for Europe."

"That's because you don't know anything about it."

"I want to be certain that you will be safe; you are too valuable a man to throw away your life as so many aviators have done within the last year."

"Haven't I told you I shall not throw away my life?"

While this seemingly pointless conversation was going on, Harvey Hamilton studied his man. He noted the tones of his voice and the expression of his face, so far as the heavy, grizzled beard would permit. The heart of the youth was filled with a kindling hope at the evidence that the Professor was mellowing. Harvey had made a favorable impression and he followed it up with rare skill.

"You say you are absolutely certain that when you start you will reach the other side of the Atlantic without mishap?"

"There is not the slightest doubt. I understand my machine better than you do."

"Not only that but a good many other facts better than I. I am so interested in you that I am going to ask a great favor."

"What's that?"

"That before you start to sail almost three thousand miles eastward, you travel the same distance westward."

The piercing eyes opened so wide that it was clear the Professor did not catch the full meaning of the remark.

"Travel westward," he repeated, as if to himself; "what are you saying?"

"It is about three thousand miles from where we stand to the Pacific Ocean; why not sail to that coast and return? If you succeed—as of course you must—no one can doubt that you will make the ocean voyage in safety."

The Professor still stared and Harvey elaborated his scheme.

"All the way from here to San Francisco, or any part of the Pacific coast, you will travel over land. Of course there will be some rivers, perhaps lakes and the Rocky Mountains to cross, but if any slip occurs you can come down without difficulty. On your return you will have the same thing over again. Don't you see what an admirable training it will be?"

The response to this question fairly took away Harvey's breath.

"Will you go with me?"

The young aviator cleverly parried the stroke. Assuming a coy expression he laughed:

"This is so sudden, Professor."

Then he removed his eyes from the face of the man and looked down to the ground as if considering the question.

"Wouldn't that be glorious? Will you really let me go with you?"

"I'll start this minute if you will be my companion."

"Confound it!" exclaimed Harvey impatiently, as if angered at the thought; "that brother of mine—the fellow with the Winchester who treated you so mean—will be sure to put in his oar. He is very fond of using that rifle of his and he shoots mighty straight."

"What of that? We can rise far beyond range of his weapon."

"And then, there are my father and mother; I don't want the governor to have an excuse for bringing out that hickory gad in the woodshed."

"Why will he object?"

"You know how a good many fathers are; they seem to enjoy butting in and stopping the fun of their boys. I shall have to skip down home and get father's consent before I dare start. I'm awfully obliged to you, Professor, but fear I shall have to wait till you come back from the Pacific coast. How easy it will be for me then to go to the governor and remind him that since you have made the six thousand mile journey safely, he can't refuse to let me go with you across the Atlantic. That's the scheme, Professor; what do you say to it?"

Professor Morgan stood for a moment in deep thought. Suddenly he raised his head and said with startling earnestness:

"I'll do it!"

CHAPTER XXVI
THE END OF THE DRAGON

"GIVE me your hand on that!" exclaimed Harvey Hamilton, impulsively, stepping forward. Professor Morgan met him half way, for he had been completely won over. The change of mood on his part was almost incredible. The young aviator had gained a remarkable victory.

"I have been so delayed," said the elder, "that I'm not willing to lose another minute."

"Why should you? I shall give myself the pleasure of seeing you start and wishing you the best of luck."

The inventor's delight was childish. He chuckled and boasted of the sensation he would cause when, at the end of a week, he returned from the Pacific coast, and picking up Harvey Hamilton skim away for the other side of the Atlantic.

"And you will go with me sure, young man?" he asked, after seating himself in his monoplane, looking wistfully down upon him.

"Just as sure as I secure my father's consent,—you may depend on that."

"I shan't forget it."

Seated at the front the Professor glanced sharply around. The package of supplies which he had gathered at the hotel in Dawson was secured on the seat behind him, and the controls which governed the uplifter, the searchlight, the rudders and motor were found in perfect trim. Nothing remained to be done except to call a cheery good-bye to the friend whom only a little while before he looked upon as his most execrated enemy.

Harvey swung his cap and never were more hearty good wishes shouted to a voyager than he sent after the inventor, who turned his monoplane westward, as if the course was as familiar to him as that between Purvis and the points immediately surrounding it.

The young aviator stood watching the helicopter as it sped away, until it became only a flickering speck in the distance and then faded from sight.

"Poor man!" sighed Harvey, "I wonder if I shall ever see him again."

He never did. Somewhere in those impressive solitudes, Professor Milo Morgan and his Dragon of the Skies met their fate. On that summer day in 1910, when he steered the astonishing product of his brain toward the setting sun, he passed into the great unknown, from which he will never return. He was only one of the martyrs whose numbers must be added to before the problem of successful aviation will be solved.

Now that he had taken himself out of the affairs of Harvey Hamilton the latter stood for a long time, wondering, speculating, hoping, and yet fearing what the end of it all was to be. The inventor in his haste had not even paused to close the door of his workshop. Harvey gently shut it, but observing no lock, he walked to his biplane and a few minutes later was at the home of Aunt Hep, where he had dinner with her and Ann. When he had told his story of the departure of Professor Morgan he made a proposal.

"I want to surprise your brother, of the Washington Hotel at Dawson, by taking both of you with me. This you know will be only a call, and I can bring Ann back to finish her visit."

"I never can think of it," protested the elder lady.

"There's no need of thinking of it; come on."

The good woman shook her head and remained obdurate, but in the end she yielded; the two passengers took their seats, and if there was ever an astounded man it was the landlord, when the aeroplane settled to rest in front of his hotel, and springing lightly to the ground, the young aviator helped out the ladies.

Not only was the man amazed, but he was indignant. He declared that the two had taken their lives in their hands and done the most tomfool thing ever known. Ann's declaration that she intended to return with her aunt by the same vehicle that had brought them thither was met by an emphatic refusal. The daughter was forbidden ever to repeat the act, and though she pleaded and whimpered, she was ordered into the house, there to stay until her "paw" allowed her to step outside. Harvey had made a mistake in counting upon the consent of the parent. So, perforce, he bade Ann good-bye and returned with her aunt, who was safely deposited at her own door.

His next proceeding was to sail to the camp on the shore of the lake, and rejoin brother Dick, Hunter, Wadsworth and Bohunkus Johnson, who as may be supposed were consumed with curiosity to learn what the flight of the monoplane and its owner meant. They had seen it heading to the westward and could not guess the explanation. They soon had the story from Harvey, who blushed at the compliments he received.

"I'll admit that you are ten times wiser than your big brother," said Dick; "for you did the only thing that could avert the gravest peril."

"There can be no question as to that," assented Hunter; "the Professor was boiling with rage and revenge and he would have done terrible things with those torpedoes of his."

"But he is out of the running now," commented Wadsworth.

"I wonder," continued Dick, "that he did not attack you the minute you came within reach."

"I think he would have done so had he not seen I was armed. I took care that he should know that. You had already given him a good scare with your Winchester and he had no liking for my smaller weapon. I fell in with his views or seemed to, and he was won over. I gave him my promise that when he returned from the Pacific coast I should go with him across the Atlantic, provided father and mother consented."

"A mighty safe promise to make."

"Am yo' gwine to take dat trip to Afriky?" asked the grieved Bunk.

"Yes, when I can gain the permission of my parents."

"How 'bout me?"

"It's the same with you; if Mr. Hartley says yes, you can go with the Professor."

"But yo' told me he's crazy; how 'bout dat?"

"So he is; do you think my people will allow me to do as you did?"

The truth filtered through the brain of the colored youth. He held his peace and listened to what the others said.

The most natural sequence of the incidents narrated was that since none of the three had ever ridden in a monoplane, they should decide to indulge in the experience. Dick Hamilton, without the least hesitation, climbed into the rear seat and settling into position with his hands grasping the supports, called upon his brother:

"Let her went!"

Bunk assisted in starting in the usual fashion by setting the propeller revolving and holding the machine back until the "auspicious" moment, while the three who stayed behind watched the flight, which proved more thrilling than even Harvey expected. When only a few hundred yards away and before much of a height was reached, the biplane dived into an aerial pocket or maelstrom, which came within a hair of making it turn turtle. The young aviator had no thought of anything of the kind, and for the instant was unprepared. The huge wings flapped like those of a mortally wounded bird, it reared and then dipped on the right, until in a twinkling it stood almost vertical. The spectators held their breath, certain that a frightful tragedy was going on before their eyes. Dick Hamilton believed the same, and held on as he had done many a time when executing the giant swing in the gymnasium. Instinctively he swung as far as he could to the left; Harvey did the same, raising the right ailerons and lowering the left, and drove ahead. It was the only thing that could save them. As it was, when the machine shot through the furious swirl into the calmer stratum beyond, it still wavered, shook and leaned over so far that several minutes passed before it was brought back to its horizontal position.

Harvey glanced over his shoulder at his brother, who smiled back, but his face was as white as a sheet and he decisively shook his head. He did not like it and longed to be back on firm ground. He did not shout, but had the good sense to know that

Harvey understood the situation better than he and would meet it as best he could.

In its descent the biplane had hardly touched the earth and was still running when Dick made a flying leap from his seat.

"Thank the Lord!" he exclaimed; "I'm with ye once again. No more for me!"

His friends laughed and rallied him. But he was insistent.

"Terra firma is good enough for me; you may try to reach heaven before your time, but I'm through."

Then Wadsworth suggested that Hunter should take the next turn. The Southerner couldn't rob his friend of the honor; he would wait until his comrade had enjoyed the treat. In the end, though, Harvey and even Bunk joined in urging them to accept Harvey's invitation, they sturdily refused, because of what they had witnessed a few minutes before.

Harvey stayed through the next day in camp, hoping to overcome the fears of the two, but did not succeed. Even Dick held out and the young aviator ceased his urgings. He and Bunk went on several tramps and had some hours of fine fishing. Then they bade their friends good-bye and headed southward down the Hudson. They replenished their gasoline and oil at Albany, again at Poughkeepsie, as Glenn Curtiss had done before them, and by easy stages finally landed at their home near Mootsport. Harvey had sent a telegram from Albany to his father giving him the news of the rescue of Bunk, so the arrival of the couple was expected.

Bunk was distrustful as to the reception that awaited him, but Mr. Hartley was as sensible as his neighbor and did not utter a word of reproof. They understood the slow-witted lad better than he did himself.

And here it is well to close our story. Harvey and Bunk made other excursions, some of which were attended by interesting experiences; but enough has been told. Throughout the weeks that followed all waited anxiously for news of Professor Morgan and his helicopter, but as has been said none ever came and as the months passed all doubt of his tragic fate was removed.

Dick Hamilton returned to Yale in due course, but secured a short leave for a visit to the Adirondacks early in October. His heart was set upon procuring those magnificent antlers which had been within his grasp more than once. He hunted persistently under the lead of Guide Akers, but was obliged to go back to the university disappointed. In his letter making this known to his father he said:

"I have established one astonishing fact in natural history: the deer and other big game in Maine, the Adirondacks and elsewhere know exactly when the close season ends and they govern themselves accordingly. That buck last summer continually got in front of me, was as tantalizing as he could be even to the extent of grinning at me, knowing all the time that I daresn't harm a hair of his hide. Now that it is the open season, you might run a fine tooth comb from one end of Essex County to the other without bringing him to light. If I stay here until November 1, he will walk out of the woods at sunrise, halt twenty paces away and grin at me again. But let him beware: he may tempt me too far."

CHAPTER XXVII
BRAVE MEN ALOFT

ONE cannot help speculating upon the fascinating subject of aviation. Its progress during the past few years, the advancements of every day and the certainties near at hand lead us to wonder what kind of airship will sail down the invisible highways of the sky in the future. Danger incites rather than deters man from attempts to enter the seemingly forbidden field. Many years ago a philosopher remarked that if a train were advertised to make the run from New York to Philadelphia in twenty minutes, but that it could carry only fifty passengers, of whom one half were absolutely certain to be killed on every trip, not a seat would be vacant when the start was made.

On the last day of the year 1910, Arch Hoxsey at Los Angeles, and John B. Moisant at New Orleans, two of the most daring and successful aviators, plunged to death while giving an exhibition of their wonderful skill. This brought the death list for the year up to forty, and more than likely ere these lines are read the fatalities will be increased. None the less the development of the aeroplane will go on: With what result?

Well within the present decade aeroplanes will easily fly from the Atlantic to the Pacific; express and mail carriers will deliver quickly their packages to the corners of the earth; a speed of two hundred miles an hour will be attained, so that a man may take breakfast in New York and on the following morning do the same in London or Paris. An automatic stability device will render accidents well nigh impossible; aeroplanes will become as numerous and cheaper than automobiles; merchants and day toilers will have their domestic machines in which they will go to and return from their places of business; very soon the electric aeroplanes will be operated by wireless transmission of power, and will become active in war, both as scouts for the army and navy, and through their appalling power of destruction compel nations to remain at peace with one another.

No one is so well qualified to guess the near possibilities of aviation as those who have already been successful in that field.

"The air is the only element conquered by man," said Glenn Curtiss, "in which the speed promises to be limitless. The improvements that are being made daily will bring a marvelous increase in swiftness of travel. I have no doubt that two hundred miles an hour will be as common as is one-fourth of that rate on our railways.

"This development will be wonderfully assisted by the army and navy. The aeroplane will be a decisive factor in warfare. Not only will it be invaluable for scouting purposes and for carrying messages back and forth, but it will be an awful engine of destruction. A fleet of aeroplanes could annihilate New York in a day. Soaring in the sky, safe beyond rifle or artillery range, it could sound the last trump for the proudest and most populous city in the world.

"Beyond scout duty I do not think the machines would be of much help to the navy, but when the battleships attack a fortified city, they could send aloft a score or more of aeroplanes which could blow all the forts to fragments with dynamite."

It is the belief of Hubert Latham that both the monoplane and the biplane will exist in types of the airship of the future. He says that each embodies essentials that are lacking in the other and that are necessary for the proper navigation of the air.

"The aeroplane is perfected even more than people think," said he. "I could fly practically to any place that a train can go and to many places that it cannot go. If a good prize were offered I should agree to cross from Los Angeles to New York. The airship of the future will be commercialized. It will practically do all of the express, mail and parcels post business. It will be the touring car par excellence for those who wish to see the world. It is being simplified and with an automatic stability device which I think is coming rapidly, it will be every man's machine. They do not cost much and this will be greatly reduced during the next few years. It will make a better race of men and women when they fly. They will be healthier and will have a clearer idea of things as they are. I do not look forward to any great change in the type of machines and think the engine and the stability device will absorb the attention of the inventors and manufacturers of the future."

As might be supposed, Eugene Ely, the first aviator who ever flew from a man-of-war, has decided ideas of the coming aeroplane. He does not believe the airship will be very effective in dropping bombs on warships, but no one can imagine its terrible power for destructiveness for armies and cities. Mr. Ely said:

"I can carry about 350 pounds of the highest explosive known to mankind at present. Imagine that I was successful in dropping this explosive on a warship of the enemy. What would happen? Nothing. But listen to this. In Hampton Roads we tried the experiment of placing 350 pounds of nitro-glycerine against the armored side of the turret of the Puritan. It was set off and it was discovered that not even the sighting mechanism of the turret had been injured. So you see that even if we were successful in hitting our mark we could do little damage. But imagine this great explosive dropped into the midst of a regiment of soldiers. They would be annihilated in a second. If it was dropped on the roof of a skyscraper in a city, what would happen? It would be demolished in a trice. So cities are at the mercy of an army equipped with aeroplanes, and the development will be along this line."

"I have seen trials of wireless transmission of electricity and I firmly believe that the future will see aeroplanes operated by this wireless transmission of current, and then the greatest problem of all, the engine, will be solved. With electric motors we could attain a speed which sounds foolish. We could get a lifting power from the speed which would carry hundreds of pounds. The machines would be made smaller and if they had folding wings they would be no longer than the ordinary business man's automobile. With these machines he could annihilate distance and a friend living a hundred miles away would be his next-door neighbor.

"The perfection of the flying machine will mean a greater rural population, as has the automobile. It will be possible and comfortable to live a hundred miles from the city and observe business hours there."

P. O. Parmalee, who drove the Baby Wright Flyer at Los Angeles, is certain that the coming aeroplane will do all express, scouting, mail carrying and will even transport light freight.

"With my Wright machine I can take up 500 pounds beside myself, and go anywhere that I want to. If I double the engine capacity of my machine and double the wing space I can carry 2500 pounds, so I think that the future aeroplane will be a larger affair for commerce and a smaller one for pleasure and touring.

There will probably be some sort of wing adjustment which will enable the flyer to start from the ground with a wide wing area, and after he has attained his height and speed to reduce gradually the wing area and make greater speed, and when he desires to alight extend his wing area to its limit and land easily.

"I predict that within a year a great deal of the government mail, parcels post and express matter will be carried to out-of-the-way places by aeroplane. Motors are being perfected every day, and steering and stability devices are becoming better, so that the everyday man can soon fly a machine as easily as he can steer an automobile. Speed will be a great factor in the aeroplane of the future. The Baby Wright, which was wrecked at Belmont Park, was the fastest thing that man ever flew in. It made ninety miles an hour and could do better. The matter of speed has been solved for the ordinary use of an aeroplane. It is to the lightning service required by mail contracts that attention is now directed."

James Radley, the English aviator, is also optimistic of the future. He says that no one can foretell the astounding developments in aviation that are near at hand. He believes they will be along the lines now laid down, that is, the monoplane and biplane. "I can only guess," said he, "the improvements that will come in motors and steering. The machines are able to accomplish much more than has been asked of them so far. I do not think folding wings will ever be used, since the trend is toward simplicity instead of complicated contrivances. Automatic stability will be attained and it will bring the solution of the greatest problem that confronts amateurs. Within three years aeroplanes will become as common as automobiles."

An unexpected field for their use was brought to light at the aviation meet at Los Angeles in January, 1911, and was suggested by the great flight made by Eugene Ely to the United States cruiser Pennsylvania. This proved that hundreds of lives can be saved every year by the use of aeroplanes at life-saving stations or at government lighthouses. Multitudes have been lost because ships have been stranded on sandbars or rocks, where the inhabitants of towns had no way to get a line far out to them. An aeroplane could run ten or fifteen miles in a few minutes carrying a reel of cord from shore and the waves would be easily cheated of their prey.

As proof of this claim the case of the Czarina may be quoted. Early in 1910, that great ship went on the bar at Coos Bay, and forty-seven lives were lost. The air was calm and the sun shone out, but the enormous swell pounded several lighthouse boats to pieces and death won its appalling victory in the presence of thousands on the shore who were helpless to raise a hand to save them. A biplane could easily have gone out to the vessel, carrying cords which would have been the means of putting a breeches buoy into operation. Nautical men say that if the use of aeroplanes in lighthouses or life-saving stations is begun hundreds of lives will be saved every year.

Wilbur Wright, than whom no higher authority in aviation lives, thinks the world has grown too optimistic about the possibilities of travel by aeroplane. He said in Washington in January, 1911:

"It will be nearer two thousand years than two when we shall be able to fly from Washington to New York in an aeroplane in two hours. It is almost impossible to estimate the speed that can be attained by a flying machine. I would undertake to build a machine that could fly at the rate of a hundred miles an hour, but I would not want to operate it. Many years will elapse before the aeroplane will be used for transportation. It cannot supply the requirements that are furnished by railroads. Its greatest use lies in the field of sports and military operations. Flying through the air is a great sport and no more dangerous than automobiling.

"The tragic deaths of Hoxsey and Moisant, I presume, may retard the development of the aeroplane to some extent, but it will go forward. Public sentiment and laws will minimize the danger of the flying machine. These influences will check the recklessness of aviation."

And now let us wait and see to what extent these prophecies will be fulfilled.

THE END